From The Women's Press Ltd
34 Great Sutton Street, London EC1V 0DX

Yūko Tsushima

Yūko Tsushima's reputation as one of Japan's most remarkable young writers is based largely on works of short fiction. She published her first short story while at University; nine volumes of her short stories have appeared to date. In addition, she has published three full-length novels, *Chōji* (1978), *Moeru Kaza* (1980) and *Yama o Hashiru Onna* (1980). *Chōji* (*Child Of Fortune*) won the 1978 Women's Literature Prize in Japan.

Yūko Tsushima was born in 1947, the daughter of the famous Japanese novelist Osamu Dazai who committed suicide in 1948.

Yūko Tshushima lives in Tokyo with her daughter.

Yūko Tsushima
Child of Fortune

Translated by Geraldine Harcourt

The Women's Press

First published in Great Britain by
The Women's Press Limited 1986
A member of the Namara Group
34 Great Sutton Street, London EC1V 0DX

First published in book form in 1978 by Kawade Shobō Shinsha under the title *Chōji*

This translation first published in English by Kodansha International Ltd, Tokyo, and
Kodansha International/USA Ltd, 1983
Translation copyright © Kodansha International Ltd 1983
Publication of this translation was assisted by the Japan Foundation

British Library Cataloguing in Publication Data

Tshushima, Yūko
Child of fortune
I. Title   II. Chōji. *English*
895.6'35 [F]   PL862.S76

ISBN 0–7043–5017–3
ISBN 0–7043–4040–2 Pbk

Reproduced, printed and bound in Great Britain by
Hazell Watson & Viney Limited,
Member of the BPCC Group,
Aylesbury, Bucks

"Hark, my distant, quiet friend, and feel
Your breath still enriching this emptiness."

Rilke, *Sonnets to Orpheus*

INTRODUCTION

The aura of long-suffering that so often surrounds Japanese heroines is absent from the novels of Yūko Tsushima. Kōko Mizuno, the contemporary woman portrayed in *Child of Fortune*, is neither pliant nor altruistic; the kind of behind-the-throne influence enjoyed by her matronly elder sister is not for her.

Kōko's resistance to conformism is, at first, largely passive, for she is isolated, vulnerable, and ridden with conflict. While she takes pride in a certain self-sufficiency, she has arrived at it by passive means: her marriage was initiated by her pregnancy, her husband initiated their divorce, and her financial independence she owes in part to a small inheritance. She finds herself becoming increasingly isolated when her adolescent daughter is drawn away to the more conventional comforts of her aunt's family; but Kōko makes little visible effort to stop her.

Having drifted through a recent affair, Kōko begins to suspect that she is pregnant; only then does she rouse herself. Driven to escape the hold that her relations with men have always had over her life, Kōko examines her past with—ironically—obsessive urgency. She asserts herself by choosing to keep the baby, but this decision proves to contain a deeper irony. When she does, finally, declare her independence, it is with no clear idea of where she will go from there—only the certainty that she herself has changed.

As this synopsis suggests, *Child of Fortune* is part of a movement in women's fiction seen in Western countries over the last two or three decades. To read it primarily as a feminist novel, however, is not always satisfying, for Yūko Tsushima often touches on these issues tangentially, while developing other themes.

Naturally, the social issues themselves must first be understood in the Japanese context. To readers in Western countries where abortion law reform has remained actively controversial throughout the 1960s and '70s, the passage in which Kōko decides to keep the baby may appear recognizable as an anti-abortion statement, with all that that implies; and yet Tsushima is not concerned, here, with the same aspect of abortion. (In fact, though personally opposed, she believes the decision should be the individual's.) What she is questioning here is an uncritical yielding to the strong social pressures against single motherhood. Abortions are readily available in Japan under a maternal health clause—which includes economic grounds—of the Eugenic Protection Law enacted in 1948. That this legislation was a population control measure, and not the recognition of a right to abortion, has been underlined by repeated moves to repeal the economic provision once the standard of living improved. When *Child of Fortune* appeared in 1978, however, this campaign had been inactive for several years; thus the political debate was a less important factor underlying Tsushima's treatment of the subject than it would have been in, say, the United States.

The heroine's age is emphasized: to the author, thirty-six represents the point at which the full weight of social pressure or "common sense" makes itself felt. Not so very long ago, thirty-six was literally "middle age" in Japan, and such a late pregnancy would have been an embarrassment even to a married woman. Today, social expectations (a woman's employability, for example) are closely linked to age, and this contributes to the sense of isolation awaiting Kōko once she drops out of the mainstream.

The author is more concerned, though, with the part of an individual that "continues moving outside an age frame." In the complex inner life she creates for her character from layer upon layer of memories and dreams, Tsushima often finds the child unchanged in the grown woman. She has made the comment on a later novel whose viewpoint is that of a ten-year-old (*Moeru Kaze* or The Burning Wind [1980]) that love, hate, and the awareness of life and death are present as intensely in a child of that age as in an adult of twenty. As much as *Child of Fortune* is about growth, it is also about what the author terms "the part of a person unrelated to the passage of time."

Yūko Tsushima published her first short story in 1968, the same year that she graduated from university. Early recognition came to her as the daughter of novelist Osamu Dazai, who rose to extraordinary celebrity in the immediate postwar years with *The Setting Sun* and *No Longer Human*. Dazai committed suicide in 1948, and Yūko, then only a year old, has no recollection of him.

By her late twenties Tsushima had gained serious critical attention in her own right with several prizewinning volumes of short fiction. *Child of Fortune* is the first of three full-length novels to date, and the only one translated into English.

Like a number of her works, *Child of Fortune* introduces the figure of a mentally retarded boy. This character parallels Tsushima's own brother, who died when he was fifteen and she was twelve. She refers often to the influence of her early years spent in his company.

The autobiographical elements this work contains have been further developed in a series of short stories, *Hikari no Ryōbun* or Realm of Light (1979), which portray a newly divorced woman's life with her small child, but which, unlike the novel, are in the first person. In her frequent first-person writing, Tsushima is in the tradition of the highly subjective "I-novel" genre which has dominated modern Japanese fiction. In *Child of Fortune*, however, the third-person protagonist takes on a fully realized character which the author regards with detachment, wry humor, and a degree of coldness.

A distinctive feature of Tsushima's writing is the radiant imagery with which she throws into relief a life grounded in domestic detail. *Child of Fortune* becomes an exploration of "the reality of illusion"

—the limbo between sleep and waking, the distorting mirrors of dream and memory, and the power of autosuggestion. The author writes: "If the ancient Egyptians lived and died in the belief that the Nile was the center of the universe, then perhaps our present-day universe is an equally organic product of the modern imagination. . . . This led me inevitably to the novel's pseudoscientific opening passage."

The flight of the imagination above the plane of day-to-day existence found further expression in *Yama o Hashiru Onna* (Woman Running in the Mountains). In its minute detailing of the heroine's daily grind this work (published serially in a major newspaper during 1980) is both easily accessible and yet demanding; in her perspective on these events, Tsushima proves again to be one of the most exciting young writers in Japan today.

The language of Yūko Tsushima's experience is a universal one shared with women writers in many parts of the world. In *Child of Fortune* she has brought to life a character whose psychological complexity reflects the meeting of Japanese fiction and women's changing consciousness.

To end on a personal note: the novel was first recommended to me by a friend long active in the Japanese women's movement. To Sachi, and to Leslie Trainer, Mariko Morisawa, and editor Stephen Shaw of Kodansha International, I should like to express my thanks for helping to make this project a pleasure as well as a challenge.

Geraldine Harcourt
Tokyo, 1982

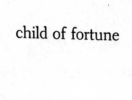

child of fortune

1

... Earth's primeval atmosphere was not yet, as it is now, "homogenized." It was as though sheets of glass of every shape and size glided there in shifting, grating masses. Some portions were too dense, others rarefied almost to a vacuum. Though frozen in some places, in others it boiled. Under these conditions it was almost impossible to judge the correct form of objects on the planet. What was actually a sphere might appear now as an elongated cone, now a parallelogram, now a rod; it might even be seen to sway limply like a strand of sea grass. Over hundreds of millions of years, however, the air eventually homogenized and these aberrations in the refraction of light disappeared. Only then did creatures with two eyes first walk the Earth. ...

Kōko concocted this explanation herself as, in her dream, she stared intently at a sharply peaked mountain of ice. It was transparent, exactly like an inverted icicle, in brilliant outline against a blue sky. Kōko knew at once what she was seeing: it was like an image mirrored there, and that was why it dazzled so. No, she thought, for all the beauty it has to offer, the primeval atmosphere isn't easy for human beings to bear. Yet she was not in any great pain herself, she was only a little chilly, and her chest felt constricted.

The dream consisted simply of staring at the ice mountain. It had no beginning and no end. When she opened her eyes the mountain was there, and when she closed them it was gone. Cold and abrupt, it wouldn't allow her emotions free play like any ordinary dream.

The primeval atmosphere, and the fact that this transparent mountain was Mount Fuji: these two things were fixed in the dream like chains binding Kōko's body. A flawless Fuji—it had to be so, though its contour was nothing like the real mountain. She was sure the atmosphere accounted for the way it looked; more likely, though, "Fuji" had been the only name to come to mind when she faced a transparent mountain that had existed since time immemorial. She marveled: there really was no denying Mount Fuji's beauty. Her body didn't move; she didn't even feel like moving. Her ears were numbed by the enveloping stillness, a silence clearer than human senses had ever known: Kōko perceived it as cold.

It was Saturday morning. Saturday was the day her daughter Kayako came to stay. Kōko dressed quickly, still turning the brief dream over in her mind.

When she opened the heavy metal door, the milk carton on the step caught her eye. It was marked with the English word "Homogenized." The dream had lacked the special texture of a nightmare and yet now that she was awake it left her very uneasy. The uneasiness receded in the crisp morning air, to leave her feeling vaguely unsatisfied.

On Saturday afternoons, after school was out, Kōko had to hear piano lessons, five very young pupils at a time for an hour each. She would work her way along the row of five rooms, listening to their Hanon, their Bach, their Burgmüller, with a word of advice for each one—lower your wrists, your right hand is too heavy, keep the tempo slow—until she could no longer tell the tunes apart. Wearily she would motion a child aside, play the set piece herself, and send the children home with instructions to practice the same thing for next week. They were happy to go. Not one of her pupils liked the piano; in fact even those who'd enjoyed it at first came to hate it after a few sessions. This system is just too awful, Kōko often thought. But I'd never pass for a teacher otherwise. And she would avert her eyes from the children. In any case it wasn't doing them positive harm. Still, in spite of herself, she would find them gradually setting her nerves on edge. Why does that boy make such a performance of yawning? Why does that girl have such stiff fingers? They're like sticks. Could she be playing volleyball at school?

That day she allowed just one to advance to a new piéce. For a change she selected one of Mendelssohn's "Songs Without Words."

–That's not what I call a real job– Kōko's older sister had said to Kayako. –It's only part-time. What makes her think she can support herself and a daughter on her pay? If anything goes wrong she'll turn to us in the end. Which means in fact that she's relying on us all along. Of course she has to, she couldn't expect to make ends meet otherwise, so she should stop being so stubborn and simply come and live here. We'd be delighted to have her. She is my only sister, after all. Really, for someone who's thirty-seven she has less sense than you, Kaya dear.–

–That's what Auntie said– Kayako had reported to Kōko.

–I'm only thirty-six– Kōko had protested with a laugh. –And I'm getting along just fine as I am. She's always been a worrier.–

Admittedly, though, what she was doing was a bit of a fraud. She'd long since dropped her own piano studies, and though there was a piano in her apartment it was a while since she'd even lifted the lid. Her sister Shōko had always been the better pianist; no wonder she was worried. And yet Kōko couldn't bring herself to abandon something that she had carried on so far.

After their mother's death, two years earlier, Kōko had taken the advice of her sister's husband—who was a lawyer—and used her inheritance to buy the apartment she now lived in. That was enough for her. But her sister seemed troubled because the apartment had cost less than Kōko was entitled to receive, and since then she had tried to do various favors for Kōko by way of her daughter: Kayako's clothes; sets of junior classics; a microscope. She arranged for Kayako to have piano lessons together with her own daughter, and she took her to concerts.

Had all this appealed to Kayako? At New Year she had simply moved in—alone—with Kōko's sister and begun going to school from there. She explained that she wanted to concentrate on a last burst of study before the junior high school entrance exams, which were only days

3

away now, in February. –At Auntie's they don't make the children do all the stuff you make me do, Mom. When I told them how I clear up after dinner, and wash and iron my own things, and even sew on buttons, they were sorry for me. I was so embarrassed.–

Kayako had long been against going to a municipal junior high, but when Kōko asked where she did want to go she always fell silent. At the last minute she named a school, adding hurriedly, –Auntie says she'll pay for it. She says don't worry because it's really Mom's money.–

Kayako's choice was a private Catholic school, the one her cousin attended. Kōko didn't object. It would have been useless anyway, for Kayako had already put a distance between them. If this was to be the result, Kōko could only regret having let her sister and brother-in-law keep the small share of the estate that by right was hers. But then they'd have had to subdivide the land on which they were living—something she couldn't bring herself to suggest. And after she'd left all the legal ins and outs to her lawyer brother-in-law, too, it had seemed only natural not to claim her full share. This wasn't something that she could explain to the satisfaction of Kayako, still in elementary school.

Kayako now returned to her mother's apartment only on Saturday nights. She kept strictly to this schedule, arriving on Saturday evening and leaving early Sunday morning. She would set off to take a practice test, or to meet a friend, or for some such reason. Each time, Kōko felt she was being tormented for her own weakness—it was always the same, always a turned back that she was forced to look at. She wanted to keep her daughter with her on Sunday morning at least. But to tell her so might be taken as nagging, and then Kayako mightn't come near her at all. And so she would see her off with a smile; it could be worse, she told herself. It had been the same with the girl's father Hatanaka, and with Doi. But her daughter Kayako was different, Kōko would quickly add—she must be different, whatever happened.

–I suppose your aunt told you to come?– Kōko had asked on the second Saturday. –I'll bet she said you should at least show up once a week?–

4

Kayako nodded matter-of-factly. –That's right. She said we can't let your mother out of our sight or there's no telling what she'll get up to next.–

The wind had risen and the streets were hazy with dust. The sky, though, was clear and bright. Kōko remembered the perfectly clear primeval sky of her dream.

She did some quick shopping on the way home from the station. Kayako wasn't there yet when she reached the apartment. Not slowing even to change her clothes, she started to fix dinner. She had eaten nothing since the plain noodles she gulped down for lunch. Her hunger had already turned to an ache. Her appetite had been steadily growing lately, and she was beginning to put on weight: she couldn't tell exactly, without bathroom scales, but she was sure she must have gained seven or eight pounds. Yet she felt so unwell every day that she wondered if she wasn't sickening for something. Her chest would feel so heavy that she had to check her temperature, and each time she was running a slight fever. It had been exactly like this when she had Kayako. She'd been troubled by a fever and a cough which made her suspect something seriously wrong, yet all the while she was gaining weight— nearly ten pounds in less than two months. It was when she was telling Hatanaka about this that she first wondered—could it be. . . ? It wasn't as though she hadn't been aware of the possibility all along.

Now, too, that possibility had crossed her mind. As she sliced the vegetables she worked out the dates, over and over again. The last time she'd seen Osada was in mid-December: it tallied all too well. But I can't be certain yet, she told herself. Fighting down a half-knowledge of some change inside her, she went on preparing the meal. She eventually decided on a chicken dish to be cooked at the table: it would give her more time to talk with Kayako while they ate.

When the ingredients were nearly ready she vacuumed Kayako's room. The apartment had two bedrooms and a kitchen-cum-dining area. Kōko had given the smaller room to Kayako and kept the larger for herself; what with the piano, the chest of drawers, and the dressing table, however, in the end hers was more cramped than Kayako's. And so she was in the habit of spending time in Kayako's room when she wanted to stretch out and relax, as she did on Sundays. It was the only sunny spot apart from the kitchen. Its windows were still hung with curtains that Kayako had made last summer vacation, choosing the cheap cotton fabric herself and running them up neatly on her aunt's sewing machine. Their red checks made Kōko rather less comfortable there. Kayako used to buy a flower or two sometimes, when she was in the mood, to brighten her desk. Kōko would ask for a share to go on the dining table, but it was no good, she never parted with any. Now, photographs of kittens and alpine plants were still pinned on the wall, but her satchel, the things she needed for schoolwork, and enough changes of clothes for a while were gone—and with them the warmth, the breath, the smell of Kayako.

If she could, Kōko would have liked to punish Kayako during this visit, as she used to do when she was three or four years old, by taking her food away or sending her outside barefoot. At that age such measures had been wonderfully effective: between sobs, Kayako would take mouthfuls of meat or eggs. She was a skinny child who, given her own way, would have eaten nothing but fruit and plain rice.

Close on seven o'clock the doorbell rang. Kōko deliberately did not go to the door. The chimes sounded again. Then there was the click of a key in the lock.

On the spur of the moment, Kōko asked Kayako, who, having eaten nearly all the chicken, was dispatching her second bowl of rice:

"Do you remember the time we went to Karuizawa in the winter? You were only five. . . ."

Kayako paused, munching, to think for a moment.

"Where there was a lot of snow?"

"That's right. Remember, we had snowball fights."

"Mm, I remember, sort of. . . . The snow really hurt."

"It made you cry. You were so sore, after you'd played in it for ages with your bare hands."

"Didn't I have mittens?"

"I forgot yours. So I gave you mine. You were thrilled they were so warm."

"Was I?"

"Yes, and then you started right in to complain. 'How come you're the only one who's got these nice things?' You were always complaining when you were little."

"Oh, yeah? . . . Wasn't there a slide I played on, too?"

"Ah, you do remember, then? You kicked up a fuss about wanting a slide even though it was covered in snow, and in the end I let you have a go. You're the one who's in for a cold time, I thought. But you were smart enough to try it only once. The snow slid down with you and gave you a fright *and* a wet bottom."

"Mm, yes, I remember that. . . ." Kayako picked a morsel of chicken out of the pot. "But listen, Mom, the exams are next week. Next Friday and Saturday."

"Really. . . . I hope you're working hard."

"That's not the point. You have to come too, Mom. . . . Parents have to be there for the interviews. Please, will you come?"

"At such short notice. . . ." Kōko refilled her beer glass and drank.

"Mom!" Kayako's face reddened. Not hiding the surge of annoyance she felt, Kōko said quickly:

"You should have told me sooner. It's not as easy to arrange as you might think. But, well, this time it can't be helped, I suppose. . . . Just this once. . . . They'll all be rich little ladies, though, won't they? Can't say I'm looking forward to it."

"It won't be like that. . . . So, you will come, won't you, Mom?"

"I said I'd have to, didn't I?"

Kayako nodded and then, silent again, began stoking rice into her mouth. Lately she had developed a definite stoop, perhaps because she'd grown too fast. Her hair was parted girlishly down the middle and softly curled at the ends. But Kōko could only think: if this is what's

7

meant by growing up, then I wish she hadn't. Once, baby Kayako used to break into a big, toothless smile at just a glimpse of her mother's face. Now Kōko was furious with her young self: why hadn't she tried more greedily to soak up and save the laughter? If she were going to raise another child, she would cuddle it and nestle its cheek against hers for all she was worth, leaving nothing to regret.

With Kayako, she'd been reluctant even to bare her breast and nurse her. No matter how Kayako cried in the night, she never picked her up from the cradle; she wouldn't even bother to get out of bed and take a look. –It's all part of her training– she'd say knowingly to Hatanaka, but the simple truth was that she indulged herself more than the baby. Hatanaka's accusations of neglect filled her with resentment. He'd say: –Surely most mothers would naturally want to give all the energy they've got?– and she would look away from Kayako's smiling face with a show of boredom. But Hatanaka himself had been too attached to his own youth; it came before everything else. They had both been very young parents. It was only after Hatanaka moved out, and Kōko found a new apartment and began taking care of Kayako on her own, that genuine fatherly and motherly feelings had sprung up in them for the first time.

She took Kayako to Karuizawa in the spring of their second year alone. It was the first holiday she'd taken with Kayako since her father had gone from their day-to-day scene. Perhaps the morning's strange dream was still on her mind now, for Kōko could feel the dazzling brilliance of the snow on that trip, and she could have sworn it came from behind Kayako as she sat at the table.

"I've finished, thanks." Kayako rose and began clearing away the empty dishes. When the two of them were together, their roles continued just as before: Kōko cooked the meals, Kayako set the table; Kayako washed the dishes, and Kōko did her laundry. Now that Kayako lived with her aunt the laundry was much less trouble, so instead she would clean the bath or give the kitchen a once-over. But today Kōko stayed on sitting at the table. She stared at Kayako's tall, narrow back as she drank, picking from time to time at the tidbits of mushy cabbage and *tōfu* left in the pot.

As long as they could go for a trip she hadn't minded where they went. Even when they had more or less decided on Karuizawa, she wasn't expecting snow. She might actually have preferred Izu or the southern tip of the Bōsō Peninsula. She couldn't quite remember how it came to be Karuizawa. It didn't sound like Doi's idea—he wasn't the sort of man to be attracted to snow and ice. Maybe they'd come up with that hotel in the middle of the Karuizawa golf course because, with Kayako only five at the time, they had to allow for a good heating system and a menu that offered Western-style food.

Kōko had boarded the train at the last minute, leading Kayako by the hand.

–Oh, you've brought her along– Doi, on his feet watching tensely for Kōko, murmured when he saw Kayako.

–Is Uncle Doi coming too? Why?– Kayako, in turn, caught sight of Doi with surprise.

–It's better to have someone to carry the luggage, isn't it? It's so heavy– Kōko replied, handing him a sizeable overnight bag as she spoke.

–Mm, Uncle Doi is strong– said Kayako to no one in particular while her eyes followed the bag's movements. It was crammed full of her picture books, jigsaw puzzles, stuffed toys, crayons and coloring books.

For at least a month, Doi had been suggesting they go away somewhere for a break. Of course Kōko had taken to the idea immediately, but she was held back by a suspicion that he didn't mean to include Kayako. She could have simply asked him outright, could have told him she wanted to take Kayako along, and Doi wouldn't have refused. He would have said easily, as he always did: –We haven't any choice, have we?– He had already kept them company on Kayako's outings to department stores and the zoo. But entertaining Kayako couldn't have been much fun for Doi, for he had a child of his own of about the same age.

Soon after Kayako was born, Doi had come around to congratulate them with his wife and their own baby, who was crawling all over the place by then and must have been about a year old. They brought a set of quoits as a present. When she thought of the old Doi, and then of this new thoughtfulness which extended even to other people's children, Kōko sensed the weight that fatherhood must have in Doi's own life.

Kōko couldn't forget his dejected tone when he'd told her –This time she wants to have the baby.– There was no show of indifference in the words. Kōko had been concerned for the woman—who was then living with Doi—and often wondered aloud what they would do. She believed she understood pretty well, in her own way, how they'd come to live together and how sour it must have turned. And every time she saw them she would be chilled by her own reading of the situation: when would they split up?

–Well, anyway, she seems to want to have it– Doi had said. –Though she's only letting herself in for a hard time.– As soon as the baby was born, however, Doi had registered their marriage. And only a couple of months after she heard Doi's news of his girlfriend's pregnancy, Kōko herself had begun living with Hatanaka. Then when she found she was pregnant, she and Hatanaka had made their marriage official.

–Look, he's an angel, an angel. . . .–

Balancing one of the plastic quoits on top of his son's head, Doi had shared the joke with his wife like any doting father. When they were about to go, it had been Doi who picked up the boy as they took their leave.

Five years later, Kōko had remembered the fatherly figure that Doi had been then—and that even he had surely forgotten—and her heart was heavy as she looked at him with Kayako. For, astonished though she'd been at the earlier change in Doi, she had wanted to give her blessing to the small peace she saw in that new scene, not least for the sake of the woman who had become his wife.

Doi would cheerfully take five-year-old Kayako for monorail rides, fetch her bottles of pop, take her to the toilet. Seeing Kayako's excite-

10

ment, Kōko would be happy too. But on such occasions she couldn't look Doi squarely in the face. The very depth of her pleasure bewildered and shamed her, and finally left her helplessly annoyed at her own reaction. She shouldn't bring Kayako and Doi together after all, she would decide. At the time Kayako would romp around in childish high spirits, but after Doi had left she always clutched her mother's hand and held on tight. –Don't go away, Mommy. Stay with me, 'cos if you die I'll die too.– Kōko would resolve never to let Doi near them again; but that resolution never lasted for a week at a time. When she next heard Doi's voice she would go to meet him as she always did, with Kayako in tow. Always Kōko was goaded by the same greedy wants: wanting the child to adore Doi, wanting him to be loving to her.

Until just a few days before the trip, too, she'd been intending to leave Kayako at her mother's, as she'd often done in the first year or two after the divorce. Her mother shared the old house with Shōko's family, and Kayako liked to play with her two cousins. As she grew older, however, she seemed to want to spend all the time she could with Kōko. Since she was easy enough to take out by then, Kōko heeded the child's feelings and no longer left her with anyone—apart from her nursery school—if she could help it. Besides, she was growing reluctant to leave Kayako in the company of the cousins, who had a home with two parents, and a big grassy garden, and their own sandbox in the corner, and even a swing and a bar for acrobatics. Kōko was in fact proud of the way she and her daughter lived in their apartment—with no frills, and entirely on her own earnings—and she wanted Kayako to share that pride; but the cousins in their setting made a too-perfect picture. (Perhaps, she thought, it was only natural that Hatanaka, being young at the time, should have longed to fit into such a picture until faced with defeat. Partly for his sake, also, Kōko tried to stay as far away as possible from the house where she'd grown up. Though this might have been painful for Kayako's grandmother, Kayako's father clearly figured larger in the child's life.)

Before they reached Karuizawa Station, Kayako was trainsick, and after vomiting once she fell into a fitful sleep. When Kōko tried to lay her down and move to the seat opposite, next to Doi, Kayako's wails kept her at her side. She had to rest the girl's head on her knee and hold her hand. Doi cleaned up the mess with newspaper and got her a wet towel. Kōko couldn't bring herself to thank him specially, so she said nothing; Doi, too, spoke only when necessary. The coach was empty. There was no one to object when they opened a window and let in a cold breeze. Along the way they saw white birds glide down and stand motionless in the dried-out fields.

It was evening when they pulled into the station. A strong wind whipped up the snow in icy granules. Half dragged from her sleep, startled more by the force of the wind than the cold, Kayako started to cry again. They hurried through the quiet station to a waiting taxi. The windows steamed over as soon as it moved off. They felt a rising uneasiness about the hotel bookings they hadn't bothered to make since it was the off-season anyway. The blue tinge outside was already deepening.

The hotel was quiet. They were shown to a twin room, chalet-style, with its coffee-colored curtains drawn. Kōko lay down for a rest with Kayako. Doi went out to reconnoiter, as he put it—to see what the hotel was like. Whenever Doi went somewhere new, he could never settle down without first checking the place over from one end to the other. In the meantime, Kōko actually fell asleep. The night before she hadn't slept till near dawn: she'd been nervous about bringing Kayako. All kinds of scenes from the past had kept running through her mind.

She had visited Karuizawa with Hatanaka when they were first living together. In high school, too, she had once spent two weeks there with friends. Both trips had been filled with squabbles and easy, ringing laughter.

When she went there with Hatanaka—shortly after they moved in together—they had stayed in a small inn on the outskirts of the town. Then, too, it had been an off-season lull. Hatanaka's endless complaints about the shabby inn irritated Kōko. She wanted to travel lightheartedly, to take things as they came. Finally, when Hatanaka happened to invite a girl student along to their room, they began to relax and give each other gentler looks. The girl, who was staying alone at the inn, joined them in an all-night game of cards. The next day all three followed the same sightseeing route, and Hatanaka had the girl take their photo with his arm around Kōko's shoulders. Given an audience, Hatanaka was at pains to demonstrate how well he and Kōko got on together. Kōko, for her part, rather enjoyed this childish behavior.

Hatanaka resembled an actor then at the height of popularity, and his looks tended to make a good impression on both men and women. There were a few, on the other hand, who took an intense dislike to him, but he had such a circle of admirers that he scarcely needed to spare them a thought. Older people believed his prospects were brilliant, they welcomed him into their homes and made a fuss of him; younger students gathered at his feet, never doubting his seriousness. Kōko, like them, looked on Hatanaka as someone dependable, a man with a future.

From the start, she had hardly ever been alone with Hatanaka. After they'd lived for six months in the same apartment, nearly all the housewives in the building had taken to dropping in. Kōko, who didn't make friends easily, was enchanted at first by all these people popping in and out as if conjured up by some magician; but before long she found herself dreading the sight of them; when Hatanaka wasn't there she had to close the shutters by day and pretend to be out. There wasn't anyone in his crowd with whom she could talk freely, and she'd lost touch with her own acquaintances—the few she had—because they didn't like Hatanaka.

Kōko was awakened by Doi as the dining room was about to close. Kayako was watching television alone and eating her supply of candies. They hurried down, seeing no other guests in the halls, the elevator, or the lobby. Kayako kicked off her shoes with a whoop and raced up and down the deep-piled wall-to-wall carpets.

The hotel was unexpectedly large. Kōko and Doi had never heard of it before, being complete strangers to golf; in fact they mightn't have turned up so casually if they had known. At the off-season rate, or whatever it was, the tariff had seemed low enough for a leisurely stay even on the little money they could put together, and when they had phoned from Tokyo and confirmed that they could afford it, both Doi and Kōko—each knowing the other's lack of funds—had been in the best of spirits. But when she was asked if they wished to make a reservation, Kōko had replaced the receiver, unable to answer. She didn't know how many people to book for. Doi had looked happy: he was revising their budget for the trip.

In the deserted, spacious restaurant, Kōko smiled to think how excited they had been that day.

–What is it, Mommy? What's funny?–

–Look, we're the only ones here. Isn't it great?–

Doi burst out laughing. –But we can't take our time over a drink like this.–

Along the far wall stood a row of waiters surveying the three diners. Good though the food was, they withdrew quickly to their room; there they settled down with cans of beer from a vending machine.

–We always end up this way– Kōko laughed. Kayako played awhile in the shower, then came to her clutching a stuffed toy and begging for a story.

–You can read it yourself, can't you?– Doi butted in before Kōko could answer. With a glare, Kayako pressed her cheek against Kōko's shoulder and retorted:

–I'm asking Mommy.–

–What's the matter with you? How old are you supposed to be?–

–I don't care. Uncle is just an old Bugle Hound, isn't he, Mommy?–

Bugle Hound was the name of a slow-witted villain in Kayako's favorite TV cartoon. For some reason he always had a bugle slung over his shoulder.

–All right– Kōko said. –Seeing it's a special occasion. Which one shall I read?–

14

Doi gave a wry smile and held his peace. After darting him another look Kayako chose a storybook from the overnight bag.

In the end Kōko had to read all three books. Since Kayako had learned to read by herself, there'd been little opportunity for the bedtime stories with which she used to send her to sleep, every night without fail. Now she had another chance—and while she read Kōko couldn't resist flashing a dirty look at Doi's turned back every now and then. She knew it was the same look that Kayako had given him. Doi was *not* to say anything to Kayako that sounded like an opinion of her. He must never casually pass the same kind of remark he would fling at his son. Kayako—and Kōko too—overreacted. Even when Kayako plainly deserved a scolding, as soon as Doi opened his mouth Kōko would want to take her side. She was often shocked to find herself abusing Doi and stroking Kayako's head. She would realize then that she was the one making Kayako hate Doi—exactly the opposite of what she'd meant to do. But, as if he were a gumdrop, she couldn't bear to have him turn even slightly bitter to Kayako's taste.

–Well, so she's out of the way at last. Whew!– As soon as Kayako was asleep, Doi put his arm around Kōko's shoulders and drew her close. Though she couldn't take her eyes off Kayako's small black head, Kōko managed a smile for him. Why, she wondered, hadn't she thought earlier of going away with Kayako, just the two of them? Although she had Doi to thank for the fact that now, anyway, she was settled in a hotel like this, gratitude was the last thing she felt: she was irked by his very presence in the same room. If only she could go back six months: then, she'd been as thrilled as a kid on her birthday because Doi, unlike other men, wasn't discouraged from coming to see her even when Kayako was there.

Kōko and Doi slept in the other bed. Though she had meant to move into Kayako's bed by daybreak, she found herself still there on waking.

That morning they had their first sight of the glittering snow outside the window. When she tugged the heavy curtain aside Kōko felt the white light strike her bodily, and she let out a gasp. Doi and Kayako came running to the window.

–Snow!–

–I never realized it was so deep last night.–

–Look at the sky– said Kōko. They were all squinting into the glare.

–Bright blue.–

–Mommy, we can make lots of snowmen, can't we?–

–Yes, lots, all you want.–

–Ooh, I'll make a hundred. Come on, quick!–

–Not yet. Breakfast first. Oh, look, a bird, can you see it?–

There was a clump of trees and brush about fifty yards from the window, and under the nearest tree they could make out long brown tail feathers flicking up and down. Not a single human footprint was to be seen. Probably no one came near the place in winter. In this world of deep snow, the bird's long tail was like a red flame. The words "I'm so glad we came!" almost burst from Kōko's lips, she was so stunned by the dazzling brightness outside the window.

–That could be a hen pheasant– Doi suggested. –It's not a sparrow or a pigeon, I can tell that much.–

–Even a child could tell you that! But it might really be a pheasant, you know. . . . A pheasant!– Glancing at Doi's face, Kōko began to laugh. Only laughter could express the lightness of her heart. At her side were Doi and Kayako. Both were looking with sparkling eyes at the whiteness of the snow. They breathed in and out deeply. Kōko chuckled again: –A pheasant!–

–I know pheasants too. The pheasant was given a dumpling, wasn't he, Mommy?–

–That's right. A millet dumpling. . . . –

Before Kōko finished speaking the bird spread its wings and flew swiftly away. Several chunks of snow tumbled from the branches above, softly denting the snowy surface below. Neither the wing beats nor the rush of the snow reached them. It didn't occur to Kōko that the double glazing was to blame. Enraptured, she felt as if the sheer whiteness of the snow repelled all sound.

After a breakfast of coffee and toast in the dining room, they went outside. The road had been cleared, leaving the asphalt warm and dry with snow banked a foot high on either side. They rounded the corner of the hotel. The new view presented itself with the suddenness of a great mass of frozen snow descending on their heads. Kōko stopped still and raised her eyes. It was a mountain. Not a hill but a real mountain, rearing there, clear and close, so close that Kōko couldn't hold her gaze steady. When she tried a casual look, the white mountain loomed even closer, threatening to crush her in an instant.

At their feet lay a level snowfield which must have been the fairway. Fairway or field, it was all the same to Kōko. In the distance there was a single line of red pines, and to their left a row of small huts. Kōko turned her back on the mountain and ran in the direction of the huts. Letting out a pealing laugh like a scream, Kayako chased at her heels. They heard Doi calling:

–Wait! You won't get away!–

Kōko looked back and stuck her tongue right out. Gleefully, Kayako did the same. Behind Doi's thin body stood the mountain, so that he seemed to be leaning on its white bulk. He was laughing, his mouth gaping.

With her hand on Kayako's head Kōko started walking toward the huts. Though they hadn't run far she was out of breath. Steam was rising at the edges of the asphalt where it stretched away through the snow. Kayako slipped from Kōko's grasp and ran on ahead. She hadn't yet touched the snow with her hands. While she thrilled to this unfamiliar white world, it seemed she was also afraid.

Doi overtook Kōko and gained on Kayako, in the lead. When she knew he was after her, Kayako's laughter rose to a piercing squeal, a sound that traveled lightly over the shimmering snow. Kōko stopped and watched Kayako's feet skipping about on the road. Clearly she wanted to spurt ahead out of Doi's reach, but her feet were so tangled in her own laughter that she was stuck in one spot, and reduced to still more merriment at her own plight.

17

With the dishes done, Kayako was heading toward the toilet. As Kōko gazed after her, she suddenly wondered what Kayako had worn on her feet that day. If she had forgotten even to take mittens, she could hardly have fitted her out in boots before they left Tokyo, nor was it likely she'd have packed boots in the bag full of toys. But it was hard to believe the child had been walking in the snow in sneakers for three days. What did she herself have on, then? She wasn't in the habit of wearing leather shoes to travel, and she hadn't even owned a pair of boots since her student days. So that meant sneakers. Had she and Kayako gone out in the snow in sneakers? Doi had on the leather shoes he usually wore in Tokyo, that much was certain, since he had pretended to his family that he was going on a business trip. Still, why hadn't their unprotected feet bothered any of them?

Their hands had soon complained at the lack of protection. That afternoon, once Kayako had lost her wariness of the snow, they began to build a snowman. Doi was the first to give a jarring cry and leap up from the ball he was rolling. –Yow! Ow! I've got frostbite!– While she was laughing at his antics, Kayako burst into tears.

–Ow, Mommy, it hurts.– These were no ordinary tears. As she blew on Kayako's hands, Kōko finally became aware of the pain in her own, a pain that wrung her spine. Doi turned his back on them and kicked at the knee-high snowball he'd taken so much trouble to make. The ball that Kōko and Kayako had been rolling between them had barely reached half its size.

Catching Kayako on her way back from the toilet, Kōko asked: "What did you have on your feet that time? Do you remember?"

"What?" Kayako asked back, and stiffened. Her eyes were on the beer bottles on the table.

"The time we were just talking about, that trip."

"To Karuizawa?"

"Mm. Did you have boots?"

Before replying Kayako lowered herself into a chair and unrolled the sleeves of her sweater.

"How am I supposed to remember?"

"You've forgotten?"

Kayako nodded.

" . . . I guess you would—after all, it was six years ago. When you think of it, it's surprising you can remember going there at all. . . . Do you want something to drink, Kayako? What will you have?"

"Tea. It's all right, I'll get it myself. I've just learned how to make it properly. It takes a bit of trouble, but it's worth it. What about a cup, Mom? You've drunk two bottles of beer already."

"All right then, how very kind of you. Did Auntie teach you?"

"No, Cousin Miho."

Kayako was up at once to fill the kettle. Kōko recalled what the girl's grandmother had often said: she had no special ambitions for Kayako, all she asked was that she turn out to be the kind of girl who could put her heart into the cooking and the washing. -It was a sad mistake putting your schoolwork and piano first and letting you off the housework completely. It meant you simply turned up your nose at housekeeping. You can't entirely blame your husband.-

Kayako was expertly measuring tea leaves into the pot. Watching her, Kōko felt ashamed of the tea, which was a cheap brand she'd bought God knows how long ago; it seemed unworthy of those fingers. They looked pink and soft right down to the nails. They were not the ones that Kōko remembered best—the grubby fingers of a six- or seven-year-old.

"See, you're not supposed to use the water as soon as it boils. You let it cool down a bit, then pour it in slowly so that it spreads the leaves. But not too much."

"I'm sure it's much more efficient just to toss in a tea bag."

"It's not the same at all—the smell and the taste are all wrong."

"But to save all that work somebody, somewhere, went to the trouble of inventing tea bags, right? So the least we can do is use them."

"Oh, cut it out. You just don't understand." Kayako's tone was irritable. Kōko shifted her eyes from Kayako's hands: the kid still couldn't take a joke. There was a moment on that trip when, as twilight overtook them in the snow, she had teasingly turned on Kayako, disguising her voice: –I'm really the Abominable Snow-woman. I've only been pretending to be your mother all along.– Kayako's body had gone rigid and she had howled loud enough to trigger an avalanche on the distant mountainside. Her little bit of fun succeeded only in amusing Doi, who was watching them both nearby, leaving Kōko quite crestfallen. –Of course it's not true, sweetheart– she said, –there's no such thing as the Abominable Snow-woman.– But privately she was grumbling: what a dull child. She's got to toughen up.

"Here you are." Kayako passed the tea. Kōko took a quick sip and complimented its flavor. Kayako smiled delightedly and raised her own teacup to her lips.

"I think it'd be nice to go again," Kōko said.

"Where to?"

"Karuizawa."

"Oh, you're still on about that," Kayako muttered, without interest, and lowered her eyes.

"It probably hasn't changed much. I liked that forest of red pines. I never knew till then how pretty red pines can be in the snow. We had a contest to see who could throw a snowball the highest, remember? But we were put off every time because the branches kept dumping a load of snow. I was hopeless—you weren't even in the running—and he. . . ." Pausing, Kōko sipped her tea casually before asking: "Do you remember?"

Kayako gave Kōko a long look from under her brows, puffing out her cheeks. It was the way she looked when she stopped herself from talking back and submitted quietly to a scolding. Knowing her answer already, Kōko was suddenly disconcerted. She stood up and flicked the switch of the TV set on top of the refrigerator. It was an old black-and-white set, and the picture would take some time to appear.

Kōko had continued having Doi to stay until Kayako was eight. Kayako could hardly be expected to have forgotten him—no, in fact she

20

wanted her to remember. She had a feeling that if Kayako would only remember those three years when life had revolved around Doi, they might no longer seem such a wasted, pointless time. Kayako was the one person who'd always been borne on the same current as Kōko. But the recognition that she did remember Doi made Kōko afraid of the coloring that her memory might have. How much had that small child taken in? It was an eerie thought. *Why* does she still remember, when I'm sometimes on the verge of forgetting, myself? She wanted to stick her hands inside Kayako's head and rearrange its contents for her. The picture finally appeared on the TV screen: a fiftyish woman, weeping. The announcer was reporting a major fire in an office block.

"What's happened? A fire?" It was Kayako's excited voice. Kōko adjusted the set, made the picture a little clearer, then sat back in her chair. Kayako spoke again: "Wow! I wish it was in color!"

Twining flames and smoke leaped from the windows of a square building. A tiny human form appeared in their midst. It seemed to be capering about in the heat, waving both arms high.

"Where is that?" Kōko asked Kayako.

"Don't know. Wow, six people dead."

The scene gave way to the next news item.

"Which are you most afraid of, Mom: fires, floods, or earthquakes?" Kayako's voice was still excited.

"Well, I've only been in earthquakes. . . . But it's floods that really give me the creeps. I've got a thing about water. You know the sort of place where water squelches out under your feet? And it's dark, and covered in moss? I can't bear places like that for a start."

Kayako rounded her narrow, slanting eyes, and Kōko laughed. She was terribly thirsty; perhaps the amount of beer she'd drunk had only served to whet her thirst. She stroked her belly. Would another baby—if there were one—look at her with those same eyes? She was gradually noticing her own desire to reminisce with Kayako, oblivious of time. She wanted to indulge herself this way, if only for the moment.

"I'm not sure how I came to feel like that. . . . I still remember the first time I went into a forest in the mountains. It was before I started school, so I must have been four or five. I've forgotten what was going on, but I can clearly remember how it felt. It was a big forest, and even though it was summer it was dank and dark, and wet underfoot. The forest floor was bare—not a blade of grass. The trees were so tall I couldn't take them in, and I couldn't stop thinking about the earth."

"Mom?" Kayako was half out of her chair. "Mom, aren't you going to heat the bath today?"

"We'll leave it off the agenda for today. And, anyway. . . . "

"Oh, *Mom!* You're so dirty! When I told them that you only heat the bath once in three days and only change the water once a week, everyone was horrified."

"Oh? Yes, but that's the way we did it when I was a child."

"But Auntie was there too!"

"Auntie . . . was there, but she's different from your Granny and me because she's married. You don't take so many baths when you're alone."

"You're weird."

"Oh, for goodness' sake, if you really must have a bath you can heat it up yourself, can't you?"

Kayako opened her mouth, stared at her mother a moment, then scraped her chair back and headed for the bathroom. Kōko remembered glancing in there that morning: the water in the tub had been a murky white. Sure enough, violent scrubbing noises and the gurgle of the drain soon resounded through the glass door.

After finishing off her tea, Kōko started fresh on a whiskey and water. The TV news was still on. Kōko looked closely at her abdomen. Was it her imagination, or had it swollen a little more? If there is a living thing in here, she thought, it won't yet have grown as big as a little finger. She heard Kayako's muffled voice, but when she called back it stopped. The sound of gushing water flowed out of the bathroom as if to lap at her feet. She again remembered the feel of wet earth.

She'd been taken to the forest by her mother. Somewhere in its midst was the home where her older brother had been placed. Her sister wasn't with them: she would have been eleven or twelve at the time, and since it was midsummer she may have gone on a school trip to the mountains or the sea. In fact she hardly ever figured in Kōko's memories of her brother. The seven-year difference in the girls' ages had kept her beyond Kōko's range during childhood, whereas even in the limited time Kōko spent with her brother, who was two years older than herself, she knew him to be growing inside the same tight shell. They were in fact pretty much the same height and weight. Their mother treated them like twins. But her brother was congenitally retarded. He died at the age of twelve, still unable to count past ten. That was twenty-six years ago: calculating the years since her brother's death—even more than seeing Kayako about to enter junior high this spring—made Kōko feel her own age.

Kōko and her mother had headed first for a building deep in the forest. There was a tall youth with an elongated, bluish, shaven head standing outside. From the way her mother spoke to him Kōko thought he must be the "Doctor Dummy" whom her brother idolized. Yes, he had eyes like her brother's. He was an ex-pupil of the school who lived there and did odd jobs. His nose was even longer than her brother's. When he looked at Kōko his ill-tempered expression did not change. Kōko felt afraid: he wouldn't like her, she couldn't enter this world. Mixed with the fear was envy for her brother, whose days were spent happily settled at the school.

They left Doctor Dummy and turned back into the forest. The trees were all big. The earth was black. Kōko didn't know where they were going, nor why they'd doubled back. A little further on they heard children's voices. Her mother kept walking, gripping Kōko's hand.

–When you meet the teacher, say hello nicely. Tell him your name.–

She suddenly looked up to find a grown-up beaming down at her.

Kōko was pushed aside then and left alone. The unfamiliar words "treasure hunt" were shoved at her back. She looked around: there were children stretching to reach the branches, children scrabbling with both hands around the roots. It occurred to her that she should search for something, too, but she didn't know how—it wasn't like being indoors—nor even what it was they were after. So she gave up the idea of joining in and crouched down in the shadow of the nearest tree. I haven't seen my brother yet, she thought.

No one paid Kōko any attention. She couldn't tell what sort of treasure the children were seeking as she watched from fifty yards away, but the intensity of their search was frightening—the thought that they might spy her there seemed especially terrifying. And among all those eyes should be her brother's. He had only recently entered the home; their mother had been to see him several times, but it was Kōko's first visit. She'd been happily imagining the scene: her brother waiting in a field of flowers, and the pupils and teachers gathering around them in a ring to dance and sing as soon as she arrived.

Kōko stared at the ground. It was damp and dappled with gray moss. She surveyed the forest, her eyes level with the ground. The earth stretched away endlessly. Her head felt heavy, and so did her arms and legs. Her body felt crushed by the weight of the waterlogged earth. In desperation she tried to think of some escape.

And now she couldn't stand wet earth; but she couldn't be sure whether that was what had caused it. Listening to Kayako moving about in the bathroom, she thought of other boggy places she'd encountered as a child. Yes, the graveyard earth was wet, too. Whenever she visited her father's grave her feet would very nearly slip. Puddles lay on the pathways through the temple grounds. Her father had died suddenly, shortly before her brother was sent away. Though she had no memory of that period, she knew that her father had gone to live elsewhere before she was born. One day they were contacted by the police and his body was brought back to her mother's house. She had heard the story from her sister. Their father had been at the beach, and just as he breasted the first wave he had suffered a heart attack. Evidently the young woman who was with him at the time had not immediately noticed his death. Visiting his grave always gave Kōko a queer sensation.

Her mother never spoke of their father's memory, nor showed the children his photograph, yet when Kōko was reluctant to go with her to the cemetery she would flare up as if personally affronted. Her brother had gone into the same grave. And then her mother. When the urn containing her mother's ashes was placed in the opened vault, Kōko could see her father's and her brother's urns. It's getting to be quite a little gathering in there, she'd thought, and her feelings had mellowed toward the three urns standing in a row.

The graveyard earth. And the earth in the backyard of the house where she was raised. The earth of the nearby vacant lot. Children weren't supposed to go there because of an old spring-fed pond; once, they were told, a child had slipped in and drowned. The pond was small, but Kōko heard people say that it branched out underground, and she pictured the earth afloat on the water. That was why they couldn't go digging holes or poking bamboo stakes into the ground: water would come spurting out.

Kayako emerged from the bathroom. The running water continued to rumble. Watching Kayako dry her hands and feet on a towel, Kōko pursued her own thoughts: she had often dreamed about wet earth, too. There would be a garden, grassless and treeless, enclosed by a high wall. She and her brother would be playing there. When they opened the gate and went out, they found a river flowing right at their feet. No wonder the garden was so sodden, hemmed in like that by the river. Nothing particularly unusual ever happened in the dream. She and her brother were playing childish games, then they opened the gate and looked at the river. That was all, yet it left a very unpleasant aftertaste. Nothing but the gloom would remain when she awoke. She had had the same dream several times; how old would she have been? The garden where Kōko had played in real life was filled with sunlight and the season's flowers.

"You'd only make yourself dirtier in that bath. The bottom was all slimy."

"Much obliged, I'm sure." Kōko ducked her head.

"You've got me worried. Make sure you're looking nice on the day of the interview. Go to the hairdresser."

"The hairdresser?"

Kayako stepped into her room to fetch her pajamas. While there she began to check the bookshelves and inspect the drawers.

"Mm. You can look really pretty when you try, Mom."

"You don't say."

"It's true. You usually look just like a man."

"That's right, ever since you were little you've never liked me wearing pants, have you? Once you brought me a drawing you'd made of a princess and told me to dress like that."

"Did I?"

"Yes, you did. I was touched, anyway, that you'd drawn it so well." They both laughed.

"But what about you, Kayako? What are you going to wear?" Kōko got up and went into Kayako's room. Her body had begun to glow with the drink.

"A dress."

"What dress?"

Half-crouched in front of the bookcase, Kayako was looking sharply in her direction. For a moment Kōko thought over the tone she'd just used: had she perhaps sounded reproachful?

"I'm borrowing one of Miho's. Auntie says if I'm accepted she'll buy me a new one as a reward."

Kōko nodded in silence. She glanced away from Kayako and across to the TV in the kitchen. The news was over and a drama had begun. Kayako launched into a thorough tidying of her desk drawers. Kōko had visions of tying her to the desk legs with a good stout rope. Why couldn't she be satisfied with a public junior high? Why does she fall for lace frills? Accepted? If she really is accepted, then what happens? It's one thing to buy her a dress, but quite another to keep up the school fees.

–Come on, now, let me adopt her. I'm only thinking of what's best.– She heard again her sister's voice on the telephone. –If you absolutely won't come and live here, then at least let Kaya come and you can get married again to whoever you like, or go on living it up, or whatever it is you're doing. You shouldn't entangle Kaya in your own stubborn pride.–

Her sister had said this, half-jokingly, after their mother's funeral ... which would make it two years ago.

She could still hear the bath running. It suddenly occurred to her that perhaps she should talk it over with Hatanaka. But Hatanaka had two other children of his own, he was no longer father to just Kayako. Lately, she could at last meet him without any particular emotion. (In fact, though, they were meeting even less frequently than before; Hatanaka had remarried and his wife didn't like him seeing Kōko.) Kayako, too, no longer seemed to miss him as she once had.

But when it came to the point, could parent and child get by without one entangling the other? If she gave the child her freedom, before she knew it she would be dragged along herself. Kayako's life would have to remain caught up in her mother's. Kōko couldn't let her go while so much was left dangling.

The splashing sounded louder. Kayako and Kōko looked at each other. Kayako was the first to open her mouth.

"Oh no, the bath! I completely forgot."

"It's all right, I'll get it."

Kōko laid a hand on Kayako's shoulder as she started to get up, then dashed into the bathroom to find the water overflowing. The light blue tub was sheathed in a smooth, transparent film. Kōko hurriedly reached out to shut it off. Twisting awkwardly from the waist to avoid wetting her feet, she put her hand on the faucet; the water was cold on her fingertips. She felt sick, but told herself it was because she'd been drinking. She thought of the aquarium where they had gone with Doi.

–It isn't that far from here. Let's go and take a look. There are lots of snakes—you like snakes, don't you, Kayako?–

Kayako, though annoyed at Doi's little dig, had been the first to put on her shoes and hurry them along.

–Come on, quick, let's go!–

Glass windows, row upon row, gleamed with a blue light. The oxygen pumps hummed faintly but steadily in the dimness of the hall. On the other side of the glass was a world of artificial light undulating in the water pressure. Living things were growing there. They moved without weeping or crying out. A single sheet of glass separated the creatures inside and Kōko standing outside; and yet a vast distance lay between them. The pressure supported by each pane was stifling. Both Doi and Kayako were peering in delight at the various marine forms.

Kōko had later returned several times to the same aquarium, alone. She felt compelled to go and check the rows of artificial blue light. She had even learned the names of almost all the creatures they contained. Yes, even now she could still recall a few: the Nile lungfish, the pirarucu, the alligator gar. Yet she felt no special attachment to the fish that bore these names. She went expecting a creature that lived on without a name on the other side of the glass pane. And it was dread of finally finding it there in the blue light that made her seek it out.

Around that time, Kōko had said to Doi: –I think I'd like to have a pet.–

–Don't. Knowing you you'd let it die straight off.–

Doi was sprawled on top of Kōko.

–No, I wouldn't. Not if it was the right kind.–

–You might manage to keep a cockroach.–

–Don't be silly.–

–What, then?–

–It should be a living thing, but not actually alive. Preserved in Formalin. . . . Yes, if I could look at something like that every day, then maybe I'd feel as if I was looking after it. It would no longer be just a specimen. Yes, I'd like that.–

Doi rolled away and sat up on the bed.

–I don't get it. What are you talking about?–

–Kayako would like it too, I'm sure. We'd give it a name. . . . Why don't you get us one? It wouldn't have to be anything special, and I'd

28

love to have it. We'd both take good care of it . . . of the baby.–

Doi didn't answer. He went to the kitchen for a drink of water.

Doi had once told her about seeing some deformed babies in glass cylinders. He was shown them by a friend who worked at a university hospital. Some twenty cylinders, about twelve inches high, were arranged on shelves. The surfaces were kept very clean. Inside floated the whitened bodies of all kinds of babies. Some were staring wide-eyed from behind the glass. All of them, Doi had said, looked very much as though they'd forgotten they were in glass jars and were still intending to be born.

–No, they weren't scary, poor things. They simply had some abnormality which meant they couldn't live in the air outside. It was just that . . . well, they seemed so lonely, that was the disturbing part. It was as if they resented my staring at them and doing nothing to help.–

–I'd be scared, that's all– Kōko had murmured.

She couldn't see the white bodies in her mind's eye, only the round glass cylinders—those well-polished cylinders—gleaming before her. The glass itself was invisible: she saw sparkling cylinders of sharp, silver light.

2

The telephone rang at 7:30 in the morning. Already up and fully dressed, Kōko deliberately let it ring several times before she lifted the receiver. Kayako's voice sounded in her ear, running through their arrangements: she was about to come over, so would Kōko be ready and waiting?

"It's all right, take your time. Even if you get there at the last minute, you won't lose marks for it."

But Kayako came racing over fifteen minutes later, breathing hard, her shoulders and hair wetly glistening. It was a sleety, cold morning.

"With you talking like that I was afraid you'd go right back to sleep.... So you were up already, that's a relief."

"Will I do like this, do you suppose?" Kōko asked after she'd sat Kayako down. She was wearing the black suit that she had hurriedly picked out at a department store for her mother's funeral. She'd been worried that the skirt might be too tight in the waist now, but, luckily, as it had always been on the big side, she had managed to do up the hooks.

Kayako nodded, giving a grown-up smile. She was so tense that her cheeks glowed and her eyes shone with an unaccustomed softness; Kōko noted with something of a shock that she'd turned into an altogether agreeable young girl. The pale blue dress with white collar and cuffs suited her well, except that the sleeves and skirt were a little too short. (Kōko would have liked at least to alter the hem for her, but there wasn't even time for that. With her sewing it might have taken a good two hours.) Her sister's girl was small for her age—always the shortest in the class, so she'd heard. Almost as if to compensate, she did well in school and was always elected class president; at this rate, Kōko had heard Shōko say brightly, maybe they should have her carry on her father's law practice, rather than expect too much of their son. –A woman lawyer, mmm, that would be something– Kōko had answered with rare enthusiasm, only to hear her sister laugh. –Oh, no! Nothing as high-flown as that. I'm talking about taking her husband into the family as heir.– You're awfully keen on adopting sons and daughters, Kōko had thought with a rueful smile as she caught her sister's amused expression. Her sister's husband, too, had taken their family name through a form of adoption.

After she'd made Kayako a cup of instant coffee, they took the elevator down. The sleet was still falling steadily. The street, the buildings, the curbside trees, the lampposts, and the sky all seemed heavier with water than they usually did in the rain. They hailed a taxi at once, but it made no headway in the traffic. It looked as though they should have taken the train, even if it was a longer way around. To Kayako, who was staring ahead and nervously licking her lower lip, Kōko said "I wish it would turn to snow. It'd be an improvement on this."

Kayako nodded vaguely.

" . . . I used to take you to the nursery even on days like this, you know. I'm always reminded when I'm caught in bad weather. However did I keep it up, carrying you on my back or in my arms, every day for six years?"

" . . . Do you think we'll make it?" Kayako asked in a low voice.

"We've still got more than thirty minutes."

"Mm. . . ."

The car, which had started moving at last, stopped dead again. They could see the tiny red glow of a signal up ahead. Kayako sighed and sat up very straight.

"It's all right, I promise you."

"Mm. It's not that. . . . I'm sure to be asked. . . . What should I say about Dad?"

Kayako's cheeks were flushed beyond pink to the color of bruised fruit. Did she have a cold? Kōko was tempted to lay her hand on her forehead. The only time Kayako's face showed any color was when she was feverish. Kōko could generally gauge her temperature without a thermometer, from the shade of red: now it was about 39°.

"If that's what's worrying you, we aren't doing anything especially wrong, so why not simply tell them the facts?"

"But what should I say?" Kayako's voice grew smaller and smaller.

Kōko found herself lowering her own voice. "Just the facts—that your parents were divorced when you were three. There's no need to say any more and, anyway, you've given them the family register, haven't you?" Kayako nodded. "Then there's really no need to say anything. Tell them you only know what's there in the official record. . . ."

" . . . I've heard a lot of people are turned down because of their home background."

"Huh! In other words, all they care about is their fees. They want children from families who'll be good for fat donations, and never mind where the money comes from. Why don't you drop this nonsense while there's still time?"

"Mom. . . ." Kayako spoke in a whisper, her head hanging low. Looking at her from the side Kōko wondered if she was going to cry, but instead of tears she merely let out a small sigh, her features set and impassive. Kōko regretted her own childish outburst, but she couldn't help feeling, too, that Kayako's reaction was somehow not enough. She'd never had an argument with Kayako. From the time she first brought Doi and Kayako together, the girl had slipped out of her embrace and away. She was painfully aware of this now, so much later.

Toward noon the sleet turned to rain. Kōko led the way into a restaurant. Since it was near the school whose entrance tests they had just attended, they could see several other couples like themselves. One mother bowed slightly in Kōko's direction when their eyes met; they must have been together in the waiting room before the interviews, though Kōko didn't remember seeing the dark, stout woman.

Kayako hadn't said a word since they left the school. She wasn't even going to look Kōko in the face. Her downcast eyes told of the warning she was repeating firmly to herself: she must find a place to cry, she must bear up till then. In Kōko's opinion the interview itself had been a great success. The trouble, evidently, was what the interviewing nun had said as they rose to leave. Kayako had heard from her cousin that the usual formula was "I expect we'll meet again" for a pass, "Goodbye, my dear" for a fail. The interviewer already had on hand what amounted to the pass list. Her words to Kayako had been: –Goodbye, my dear.–

Her comments earlier in the interview had seemed to imply a good score in the written tests, and she'd said to Kōko, tactfully, –It must have been a struggle for you on your own.– Suddenly ashamed of the bad impression she'd always had of the school, Kōko was all smiles for the rest of the interview. Nevertheless, once she'd bowed and left the room she was struck by the knowledge that Kayako could well have failed. Never mind what the nun had said: it was a near certainty. And so she hesitated to offer any cheery optimism; in fact she couldn't bring herself to mention anything connected with the interview, not even the nun's habit.

The school buildings were old. Inside the great gates, a pupil, probably a senior, had greeted them with a deep bow. As it seemed unkind, somehow, just to pass her by, they'd asked where the exam candidates were assembling and said thank-you politely before going inside. The first-floor windows were fitted with iron grilles. They had been directed downstairs to the auditorium. There, too, seniors in beribboned uniforms were serving as guides. Kōko had seen the uniform before: her sister's daughter Miho had been wearing it, crisp and new, at their mother's funeral.

When they were ushered into the waiting room, Miho put in an appearance. It must have been recess, to judge by the noise level outside—though even so it was rather quiet.

–Sis, you're late!– Kayako called sweetly as she went out to where her cousin waited in the corridor; this must have been prearranged. The sound of Kayako's voice drew all eyes in the waiting room toward the corridor. Kōko found herself blushing. Couldn't they at least have met somewhere out of sight of the other candidates? She was dismayed: was it becoming too much for the girl to show even a little consideration?

Her thoughts turned to the interview that lay ahead of them both; intensely uncomfortable, she shifted again and again in her chair. She hadn't entirely lost hope of dissuading Kayako even now. Slowly, too, her temper was rising. Why on earth had she taken time off from work to come here? Now she would have to take next Sunday morning's lessons to pay back the teacher who was filling in for her. However did Kayako expect to repay these sacrifices?

Kōko wanted a cigarette. It shouldn't have mattered, and yet she didn't feel free to smoke. With bent head she stepped into the corridor. Kayako was alone, gazing out of the window. Across a deserted back street there was a white building, probably some sort of dormitory. She had been cold enough in the waiting room, but the corridor was even colder—her breath was misting. Kōko thought of her condition: a chill would be the worst possible thing at this time.

–Has she gone already?– When she was spoken to, Kayako finally looked around at her mother, letting her mouth droop open. Kōko asked again: –Has Miho gone?–

–... She said to give you her love– Kayako replied without expression.

Glancing away, Kōko fished her cigarettes out of her handbag.

–Hey!– Kayako's exclamation came as no surprise. Ignoring her, she proceeded to take one from the pack. At almost the same instant Kayako's fingers snatched it from her hand. Kōko studied Kayako's face: her nostrils were puffy and red. The girl turned back to the window, squinting at the light, with the cigarette tightly palmed.

34

It had been then that their name was called. Kōko and Kayako had exchanged a look, then each hastily tidied her clothes. Kayako had shoved the cigarette into her pocket.

Kayako was chewing dismally enough now to destroy the appetites of everyone else in the restaurant. Maybe, instead of bringing her to this unexciting place, she should have whisked her off to Ginza and treated her to a fancy French dinner. But let her taste her fill of bitterness over this meal, she thought. She wanted to take a mirror, show Kayako her own poor reflection, and point out the error of her choice. Look, if you go on like this you'll only make yourself more miserable. You have to compete with your own kind. If a bird imitated a fish, it would only drown. . . .

As she waited for Kayako to finish eating, Kōko let her feelings reach out directly, for the first time, toward what had begun to grow inside her. Perhaps she needn't be afraid to have the baby. Until now the very fact of being pregnant had seemed too threatening to think about. She shifted her eyes from the plates on the table to the window on her right, for fear that Kayako—though she had no reason to suspect—might read her thoughts. It was still raining, a viscous, opaque rain. The steamy windowpanes reduced the street scene to blurred shadows. The street lamps, which had come on automatically under the darkened sky, were circled by spreading blots of violet light. The air inside the restaurant was stuffy with the heat of people and the smell of food.

Having this child would mean a new member joining the family. Kōko imagined a cradle holding a sleeping baby in her home. She would probably put it in Kayako's sunny room during the day. She saw Kayako studying at the desk alongside and, when the baby cried, looking around into the cradle and gently patting its chest or picking it up. Then calling Kōko. . . .

Three people. Kōko was strongly attracted by the number's stability. Not two, not four, but three. A triangle: a full, beautiful form. There was something to be said for the square, too, but the triangle was the basis of all form. The dominant. The chord *do, mi, so*. This perfect chord had grown too familiar to move her every time she heard it, yet its fullness had a tough resilience, more so than any other sound. Between the two of them they could never form a unit that could be called a family. With one adult, one child, they could only draw a straight line connecting two points. One end was too high, moreover, and the other too low. The straight line was askew. What harm could there be in providing Kayako with another, new point? Far from doing harm, it was the finest present there could be, and she could offer it from a direction Kayako least expected. . . .

At this point Kōko had to smile wryly at her own train of thought. What amused her was not so much its boldness as its childish optimism. Really, at thirty-six! She needed to talk some sense into herself. As her sister would say, where was she going to get the money? When the baby was old enough there were such things as day nurseries, but in the meantime what did she plan to do about her job? And Kayako, at her age, was hardly going to believe in virgin birth; the untimely pregnancy meant she'd know what her mother had been keeping secret for all those years. If she did go to that school—in fact, even at a municipal school it would probably come to the same thing—the disgrace would ensure that both teachers and pupils made her first year there a torment. It was doubtful whether she would last out a year. With her aunt advising her, she might disown Kōko.

But these worries were being answered, one by one, by an innocent voice in another corner of her mind. The money: she could have her brother-in-law make over the rest of her legacy. The job: she had heard of unlicensed nurseries that accepted babies from six weeks old; and she could get Kayako to babysit. It wouldn't be difficult to have her own hours changed to evenings and holidays. Kayako couldn't turn her back on her own flesh and blood, no matter how susceptible she might be to what people thought. . . .

Without noticing, Kōko had begun to retrace the doubt and indecision she had felt when she and Doi were lovers, and to gather them onto this belly of hers, which was not yet outwardly obvious.

36

Her indecision in those days—she could tell now—hadn't really amounted to indecision at all. But at the time she'd been stifled by her own ambivalence; her mind was always somewhere else whether she was teaching the piano or listening to Kayako's chatter. Only when she saw and held Doi in the flesh would she remember that a child of his had already come into the world and was growing up; and her clouded mind would suddenly clear. How could she possibly have thought of getting pregnant? Then she could stop Doi as he whispered with the urgency of desire –Let's worry about a baby when it happens, it'll work out.– But as soon as Doi was out of sight the uneasiness would return over her own steady refusal to become pregnant, and she would begin to imagine herself having their child.

As for Doi, he was half deserting his own child to come to Kōko—and when he got there he was Kayako's captive playmate. Surely the question must have arisen at the back of his mind: why was he humoring Kayako when it was making his own child unhappy? There must have been moments on their tours of the zoo when the cruel absurdity of the situation made him wonder what on earth he was doing. Kōko couldn't help thinking so as she watched them fearfully from behind. But, fearful as she was, she wanted to give Kayako every chance of enjoying Doi's presence in her father's place.

She couldn't resist speculating on what it would be like to have a child with Doi. Not because it might look like him, that wasn't the point. She was calculating the pluses and minuses, assessing how effective the child might be. If he were told a baby was coming, Doi would no doubt accept it in his own way. Beyond that she couldn't guess. (Perhaps Doi couldn't have said what he would do either, if she had asked him at the time.) He probably wouldn't act irresponsibly, that much she knew, but nor would he come running to her. Perhaps he'd say something like "That's a tough decision, having it on your own, it shows a woman's strength." And then merely continue to visit from time to time. Kōko couldn't complain if he did. Knowing Doi's nature she thought it was the most likely reaction; it was also the one she feared most. To be told:

37

it was your own decision, wasn't it? So don't rely on other people.

Sometimes, though she knew it was silly, she even wished that Doi were Hatanaka, because then she could have safely had another baby. Hatanaka was a man easily carried away with enthusiasm in everything he did. It was this enthusiasm that had made him rush into living with Kōko when they'd barely known each other a month. And it had been the same again when they separated. Once the word "divorce" had entered his mind it fired his imagination, inspiring fantasies of a new, free life with his young woman—until he noticed that Kōko was still around and hadn't agreed to a divorce, at which point he would be angry with her for wasting time.

It was only after they parted that Kōko realized she had hated this side of Hatanaka for a long time. In fact, she was the one who was deeply glad of the divorce.

Kōko then took up with Doi again, and without once getting pregnant. But she didn't consider herself lucky. She couldn't forget that, while she was busy weighing the pros and cons, Doi's wife had given birth to a second child. To have had another child nine years after the first, she must have been pretty determined. Kōko greeted the news with scorn: what a way to hold onto her man, she thought. And yet this was precisely what she'd been contemplating herself, day after day. She had added up the personal advantages and disadvantages, hesitated and agonized over Doi's wife, until finally she had forgotten her own capacity to decide. Kōko wanted Doi as her own property. But she wanted him in order to fill a particular gap in her life and Kayako's; even if Doi had happened to comply, she would certainly have refused to make Kayako his stepdaughter. It was not unlike wanting to buy Kayako a toy.

When Doi's second child was born, Kōko had actually welcomed the change at first, turning it into the opportunity she needed to leave him, but before very long she was stricken with a hopeless frustration, until she twisted and moaned in bed; frustration at herself, at having let Doi go, at having failed to take action. If she'd shown just a little more courage that second child would have been her own. Why was her child born into Doi's household of all places, when she was the one who had clung to Doi's body in a tangle of desire? She would find herself thinking: the baby must be three weeks old; now six months; now just toddling. Whenever she saw children of a similar age in the street she observed them closely, and she delved into the child-care books she still had on hand. Though she trembled at the wretchedness of it, she couldn't stop this preoccupation with babies. It wasn't enough merely to remember what Kayako had been like when she was little—and since Kayako was then eight years old, those earlier memories were all blurred together. When she cast back, she couldn't bring the sound of a single cry into focus.

Already three years had passed since she stopped seeing Doi. She no longer followed strangers' children about with her eyes, but her regrets were still lodged like a lump of heavy metal deep inside her body. Three years had gone by and she hadn't rid herself of the thought, I've lost. As time passed she wondered why she had been so strangely afraid of pregnancy for so long. Strange that it was she, and not Doi, who had dreaded and refused. She'd had an abortion once, while in college. The father was Doi. Kōko had gone straight to a local doctor. It had seemed much simpler not to ask Doi to pay, as they weren't then on such intimate terms, and in the end she saw to it without a word. Kōko herself hadn't attached any great importance to what had happened, she'd put it down to a small slip, just one of those things. When they began to keep closer company, after they'd left college, Kōko stayed quiet about her abortion. It was almost as if she'd only cared after she heard that he was expecting the birth of his first child. Even then, though, it wasn't such a bad memory; she couldn't account for her fear of pregnancy that way.

What she did feel at the time was sympathy for the woman living with Doi, who was still free as long as they weren't legally married. So, thought Kōko, she's decided to bind herself to one man, and the man is Doi.

Quiet, intelligent Doi, whose cynicism sometimes deflated other people's dreams in what seemed a deliberate way. He was several years Kōko's senior in college, and she looked up to him, with fear as well as admiration. She didn't even begin to trust him. Doi never sought to charm women as other men did—he held her to him willfully. He would come into her room without speaking and, brushing aside her hopes of having a good talk, would pull her roughly into his arms. And then, in company, he'd browbeat her for her indecisiveness, her readiness to change her thinking if that was what her man wanted. In those days Kōko had often tried to dismiss Doi as a man merely indulging his own sensuality. When he embraced her, though, she always responded with everything she could give.

The desire that Doi brought out in her had nothing to do with their bodies, far less with their emotions. Kōko enjoyed the strangeness of it: to think that something on that level could make a man and woman inseparable. Or perhaps it's us, she thought sadly. Perhaps it's only true of us because we're alike in the nature of our desire. It's so intense that we're blinded to its worth. Since their own state seemed pitifully deformed, she naturally had to feel sorry for the one woman—of several who'd slept with Doi—whose accidental pregnancy had made her his wife. And to watch her in admiration: how strong she must be, to take on having Doi's child. (She never dreamed then that desire might be different with another lover.)

However she looked at it, her lasting terror of another pregnancy with Doi couldn't have been due to the abortion. This left only one explanation: she must have caused it herself, as she clung to the carefree quality of a momentary, evanescent pleasure and steadily refused to face the instincts that transcended their flesh. Even as she clutched Doi's body, believing she knew after all this time what it meant to love one man, she was hating and despising the instincts in her. She feared their strength. She was thrilled when he whispered –I've loved you all along.– And had answered –But I've always loved you, too. Why didn't you tell me before?– Even her marriage to Hatanaka must have been his fault, she decided, intoxicated, now that it was ended, by this sudden pleasure.

For the first time in her life she knew its value. Or so she'd thought. But pregnancy would have been a complete affirmation of those instincts. She needn't have tried to explain her fear in terms of deference to Doi's wife. She had loved Doi but failed to see any real beauty in their naked embrace. The greater the pleasure, the more she felt that her own lonely husbandless state was being flaunted before her eyes.

When she was with Hatanaka, she'd happily accepted her pregnancy because she knew they could always get married. When she was told, she'd felt as though the people at the hospital were giving her their blessing; the word "sex" had never entered her mind—another memory that forced her to admit her own sordid cowardice. For it was she who'd trampled her relationship with Doi underfoot—under the dirty feet of respectability.

Whenever Kōko's thoughts followed this course, she had to grit her teeth in bitterness at missing the child she might have had.

Last fall she'd begun seeing Osada, a friend of Hatanaka's, and this had stirred up the old, deep regrets all over again. Every time they arranged to meet she inevitably asked herself: what are you going to do this time? Although she was avoiding pregnancy, her feelings about it were unclear. Of course Osada was also afraid of getting her pregnant. But Kōko would watch their sex as if staring bleakly down from the ceiling: what a pointless thing to be doing. Then she found herself hanging back from taking precautions, ashamed of her own vigilance. She hated the idea of pregnancy more than ever; she seemed more than usually anxious to avoid it; yet in the end she was actually inviting it. It was unthinkable, and yet she could foresee it. And she could tell that if she did conceive she would want to give birth, though it would be madness at this late date. She knew it wouldn't make up for anything, yet she would almost certainly do it. And so she'd gone on dreading pregnancy all the more.

Now, with her belly actually swelling, Kōko was so unworried that it was even a letdown. Only one thing gave her pause, a slight concern—after all—about what people would think. And even that small

41

hesitation seemed unlikely to survive her highhanded view of life, for, living as she chose until now, she'd come to care little about appearances at this stage. Maybe she *was* reaching an age when it was senseless to want a fatherless child; but, precisely because of her age, she didn't want to make a choice that she would regret till the day she died. Lately she was more convinced than ever that there was no point in worrying about what people thought. She would soon be thirty-seven. The only person watching Kōko at thirty-seven was Kōko. When this obvious fact finally came home to her it was still a surprise—what a very lonely fact it was! The baby's paternity was too insignificant to worry about; she was simply going to produce another child, and that was all there was to it.

In her college days, she had heard the words *eka kṣaṇaḥ* in a lecture on Indian philosophy. The phrase had had a brief vogue among the students. It was Sanskrit for "a single instant." She seemed to remember learning that to see and to transcend the whole universe in one instant, in *eka kṣaṇaḥ*, was the meaning of "enlightenment." She had also been told that the ancient Indian concept of time closely resembled the modern cyclic theory of the universe. Yes, there was more she remembered. Over a dizzying span of years, the universe repeats its rhythm of birth, collapse, and regeneration. The phenomena of the universe, and all the time and life that it contains, disintegrate with it; for they contain no truth that passes into eternity. The world is just a great illusion flowing emptily by; we mustn't be deceived. Where, then, should we seek the truth that passes into eternity? Hidden in the present, in a single instant, is the power to shatter the illusion. In this single present instant the eyes of eternity open, eyes that can penetrate the secrets of the movements of the cosmos. . . .

She had sat in on only one or two lectures, just for fun; but she couldn't help thinking that those remembered words were now alive in her. She had only to entrust everything, utterly, to the present moment. For wasn't each instant—*now*, and *now*—charged with the meaning of the whole cosmos? During sex with Osada, there had been a moment's sensation as though she'd swallowed the movements of the celestial bodies into her own, and at that moment the celestial body in her womb must also have stirred. It was the instant of conception, a moment of grace; there was no other word for it. Why not embrace it, then? The eternal present: how sweet those words sounded! Kōko had no difficulty believing that the universe was a great illusion. Here she was, being swept along inside the illusion: there was clearly no call to think pretentious thoughts about the new life within her.

She had two facts in front of her: Kayako, who rejected her mother and was fascinated by her aunt's world; and the pregnancy. Kōko couldn't help feeling that the timing was somehow significant: she'd been given the two at once. She couldn't grasp one and throw away the other without throwing herself with it.

"Well, shall we go?" Kōko finished her cigarette and got up to leave. On an impulse she added: "While we're downtown, I'll take you to look for a blouse in Ginza, if you like. There must be a lot of spring ones in by now."

Kayako gave a faint nod and stood up, her eyes still lowered. With her hand on the girl's back Kōko steered her toward the cashier. Right now she wanted to do all she could to console Kayako, whose confidence had quite deserted her. At one time, she could have taken her in her lap like a baby, stroked her head and murmured "You poor, poor thing" until the tears stopped. Now, however, Kayako refused to cry openly in front of her mother, and her mother couldn't put her arms around her. Kōko was moved with pity for this child on whose shoulders rested the fate of growing up. Kayako's back was lean, though the backbone was solid.

Hailing a taxi in front of the restaurant, she pushed Kayako in first. By now it was raining hard and the streets were so dark that it could have been nightfall. The exam would land on a foul day like this, she thought, as if Kayako had been singled out for this bit of bad luck. (Kayako still hadn't broken her silence after they left the restaurant.) If she fixed her gaze on the window glass, the shapes in the streets vanished to leave only a pale light dissolved in water, so that the cab rode like a glass tank drifting freely on undersea currents.

All the same—Kôko dropped her eyes to her abdomen—should she tell Osada or not? Of course she had no intention of involving him as the child's father in any way. From Osada's point of view, though, it would surely be spooky to have a child of his alive quite unknown to him. And she was likely to meet him on some future occasion.

Osada had been pressed by Hatanaka into serving as a sort of go-between. Lately the messages had tapered off on Hatanaka's side also, but until two or three years ago Osada used to phone on his behalf quite frequently. The arrangement had suited Kôko, too, for she was comfortable talking to Osada; it was a pleasure to go and meet him, taking along Kayako's report cards and photographs.

By way of Osada, Hatanaka sent presents more or less regularly for Christmas and Kayako's birthday. At first, Kôko hadn't been able to tell her these were from her father; she had handed them over together with her own, without explanation. She finally managed to tell her the truth when she was no longer seeing Doi; but by then Hatanaka, in turn, was shunning direct contact with her, just as she'd been avoiding him. They still needed Osada. She learned that Hatanaka had a baby now, two or three months after remarrying—a boy this time.

–He even washes diapers– Osada had told her.

–That's just like him, isn't it?– Kôko had laughed when she heard.

Hatanaka had lavished affection on Kayako as a baby—spoiled her, even. But he always shirked the burden of providing for them financially, when this was a very real need. She wished he'd at least share the load of housework and looking after the baby, but he merely played games with Kayako. Kôko meanwhile went to her mother for money with a growing sense that all her efforts were for nothing. At night, Hatanaka would go out drinking as usual with his young admirers and friends. Often he phoned home very late. –Come on over– she'd hear him say drunkenly. –Take a taxi. Come on, just this once.– She would put the receiver back without speaking, bitterly asking herself just whose money he thought it was, anyway.

Osada used to come and see them in those days. He was an old college friend of Hatanaka's. His health had failed just before graduation, however, and he'd gone home to the country and spent two years convalescing there. He had often written to Hatanaka, and Kōko had been shown many of his letters. They were childishly straightforward, but written in a way that compelled interest in what the writer felt.

All the letters said basically the same thing: how unhappy he was hanging about at his mother's, unable to do anything because of his illness; how he longed to return to Tokyo and find a job. But he made fun of himself and his situation, and gave a humorous twist to his accounts of the local scene. How come Hatanaka, jobless and penniless like himself, had been able to marry and even have a child? It simply wasn't fair, when he couldn't get a girl into bed for the night. Then Osada would describe some new episode. His letters seemed written with the reader's enjoyment constantly in mind. Hatanaka would chuckle over every one: –Silly fool, always getting in a sweat. When'll he ever learn?–

When Osada recovered at last, Kōko was surprised to find herself looking forward to his approaching return. The impression she'd unconsciously formed was all the stronger because they'd never met, although she felt closer to him than to Hatanaka's other friends. The first time she met him face to face she was tense. She didn't want him to disapprove of her as Hatanaka's partner. When he turned out to be more highly strung than she'd imagined, she was taut and guarded, afraid that at any moment he'd detect the impurities between them. Distrustfully, she watched Hatanaka roaring with laughter and wondered why he wasn't more wary of Osada.

–Hatanaka could have all the girls he wanted– said Osada. –And me—well, at least I made him dazzle by comparison.– But Kōko couldn't relax enough to enjoy his jokes. She was sure she saw criticism of Hatanaka in his eyes.

–That's right.– Hatanaka gave another laugh. –I passed on a lot of mine, but you never got anywhere, did you?"

Osada stayed just one night, his first back in Tokyo, before moving in with a single friend. One month later he had found himself a job and an apartment. His approach to finding both was another contrast to Hatanaka's ways: he was cautious, methodical. He was a realistic young man, quite free from the kind of pretensions in which Hatanaka was tightly ensnared. And yet perhaps his approach was too cautious, for he'd had no luck with the job, nor with his marital prospects. At present, after trying a number of other jobs, he was a reporter on a small trade paper; and he was still asserting that *next* year he'd get himself a wife.

Whenever she saw them together in the old days, Kōko used to wish Hatanaka would learn a thing or two from Osada. But the scene was always the same: Osada waiting on Hatanaka. And in spite of her irritation, Kōko would catch herself behaving as Hatanaka did, letting the bachelor Osada do the dishes and help clean up.

When she broke the news of the coming divorce, Osada protested violently, and she learned that his own parents were divorced. He couldn't approve of any grounds but child abuse, and Hatanaka had never once mistreated the child, had he? If Kōko would only hold out and refuse to divorce him, knowing Hatanaka, he'd very soon be back.

Kōko nodded agreement, but she replied: –I don't have the strength. And even when we're divorced he'll still be Kayako's father. . . . Don't you think that a young enough child can go without its father and hardly be affected? And when she's older she can see him all she wants. . . . –

Osada didn't accept Kōko's arguments, and after the divorce he no longer showed her the same affection. He maintained a fixed distance; when he came into contact with her it was strictly as Hatanaka's friend. Though she missed his friendship, she was reminded also of his integrity: she felt she could rely on Osada in every way. But she never saw him unless there was some message to be relayed. They would exchange the latest news of Hatanaka and Kayako, finish their coffee, and go their separate ways.

Last fall, Osada had phoned again after a long break. He had been asked to deliver another birthday present for Kayako. Kōko was unfortunately too busy to get away during the day, but she suggested that evening or the one after, since Kayako had just left on a three-day school trip.

The next evening she met Osada at a beer hall. While she was living with Hatanaka they'd all gone out together on two or three occasions, leaving Kayako with her grandmother. They often drank together at home, too. Osada hadn't been much of a drinker, though; after a large beer he would soon drop off to sleep, wherever he happened to be at the time. Now, eight years later, Kōko noted that his limit had increased. She was lighthearted as she recalled all the things they'd said and done. Osada also talked and laughed a lot that night.

From the beer hall they went on to a small neighborhood bar, then Kōko invited Osada back to her apartment. They sat watching TV and drinking whiskey. Osada's gaze roved around Kōko's rooms with uninhibited curiosity. They talked about rents, how much she'd paid for the apartment, whether it was comfortable; they discussed the cost of living and swapped complaints about their jobs.

When the TV station signed off, Osada said –Shall we go to bed?– Kōko nodded and got up to clear the table. Meanwhile Osada began to undress.

Naked, Osada and Kōko embraced. They held each other's bodies breathlessly, like children thrilling to secret mischief out of the sight of adults. Kōko could only marvel: had people's bodies always been so warm, so soft? Since she'd stopped holding Kayako in her arms, she had forgotten the touch of another's skin. She remembered that her own body was a warm, soft being, like this. Is there anything, she wondered, that gives people more comfort than this skin touching skin? As she explored Osada's body with her face, her hands and feet, its comfortable presence—no more nor less than human—was unbearably dear to her. She wanted to give thanks for being this living creature, a human being. Like a child she clamored for more and more caresses. She wanted to make sure, with her own body, of the two legs, the genitals, the belly, the rib cage, all the human parts: why does the sheer fact that the flesh is alive—petty and even ugly as it is—convey a sense of such depth?

Having seen Kōko's expression, Osada was apologizing, over and over again, for having been remiss. –Even today, I wouldn't have realized if you hadn't invited me here. It was stupid of me—I never guessed what was on your mind, Kōko. I didn't mean to keep you hanging like that, I just didn't realize. It's not easy for a woman to make the first move, I know.–

Kōko met Osada's words with a smile, but was thinking: if only the man were a mute. She found it hard to suppress a deep disappointment at Osada's arousal—as deep as her joy at coming into contact with a human body. She couldn't relate the pleasure that she felt to the physical desire between a man and a woman. Whatever it was she wanted from Osada, if anything, it was not sex.

Some time later Osada fell asleep, snoring. Kōko sat up in bed many times in the night to light a cigarette and stare intently at his face, childish and vulnerable in sleep.

She remembered a spiteful but plausible rumor that had gone the rounds of her class in grade school. They were so young that they thought babies happened automatically when the father and mother lived together. The rumor concerned a certain pale and peevish child who, it alleged, would never have been born if his mom and dad hadn't stuck themselves together *down there*.

Something is terribly wrong if even sex like this can lead to pregnancy, Kōko thought as she stroked Osada's head with tears in her eyes. The workings of human sex—including her own—were terrifying. Kayako, too, had had her first menstruation that summer.

Early the next morning, after seeing Osada off, Kōko opened Hatanaka's present to Kayako. Her heart sank: it was a cheap dress-up doll. There's no need for him to go on buying her trinkets from a sense of duty, she thought. It wasn't that she wanted expensive gifts. But this one revealed only too clearly how his attentiveness to Kayako had lapsed. He probably never thought to ask himself, before entering the toy shop, what sort of thing a girl of eleven would like.

Later that day Kōko called at a department store and bought a hand mirror with a carved wooden back; the dress-up doll she gave away to one of her piano pupils. Kayako naturally looked forward each year to her father's presents. Kōko thought of suggesting, through Osada, that he take Kayako out for a meal from next year, now that she was starting junior high.

Two weeks later Kōko telephoned Osada. When they met, after sex she told him about this idea. –I'll pass it on sometime– he replied.

She saw Osada several times after that. They met in a coffee shop and went to a hotel. They lacked even the guilt that would have accompanied the same behavior in their student days, and soon their phone calls stopped; it was hard to say on whose side. Osada, it seemed, having convinced himself that Kōko was highly sexed, was afraid her desire might trip him up. Just as Kōko had once felt toward Doi, it seemed that while he clung moment by moment to their sexual encounters he couldn't help being repelled by the desire that each exposed there. Though she supposed Osada's emotions were not unnatural, Kōko had to admit she found them unbearably humiliating.

She hadn't seen Osada at all since the beginning of the year. No doubt the matter of the birthday treat had completely slipped his memory by now. There was also the subject of her pregnancy. She probably should see him once in the near future—and already Kōko was starting to consider when. It didn't look as though she could carry off the feat of giving birth to a child fathered by Osada, not letting him know, and continuing to see him as if nothing had happened. It would be awkward, though, if he worried and fussed. It might be better to tell him after it was too late for an abortion. . . .

They were getting close to the Ginza. As she took her purse from her handbag, Kōko bit hard against her lower lip. It was Doi's child she'd wanted to have. How could she have deceived herself?

Because of the weather she had the taxi take them to a store at Sukiyabashi, though she knew the traffic would be slow. It was evidently intending to rain solidly all day. Not surprisingly, there were few people about in the streets. At least when it starts to rain like this it means spring is almost here, thought Kōko as she held her umbrella over Kayako stepping out of the taxi behind her.

3

Mendelssohn's "Songs Without Words" was not a wise choice. Kōko wanted to block her ears, turn on the girl whose chocolate-smeared fingers were fumbling over the keyboard, and drive her out of the practice room. They'd been on this piece for almost a month now and still the girl's fingers came nowhere near hitting the notes as they were written. She was forever making the same mistakes in the same places, and not even looking ashamed of herself. Perhaps the piece didn't agree with her, since she was supposed to have a little more ability than the others. Kōko was thoroughly sick of teaching it, and for the last lesson or two the pupil had been squirming with sheer boredom as she shifted her fingers about.

"Well, that's it for today. Be sure to look at the music carefully, now, when you practice. It doesn't matter if you play slowly, as long as it's correct.... And another thing, next week, don't you come here with such dirty fingers. Wash your hands properly first.... Goodbye."

With a mumbled goodbye the girl slipped from the room. Every one of the children came and went in the same way. "Goodbye" and "hello" were all they said; if they had to answer otherwise they spoke only in whispers, and then only to say "yes" or "no." As Kōko talked on, all by herself, they gazed up at her derisively: fancy anyone caring about this stupid old stuff! These looks would drive Kōko to even greater loquacity.

After stretching hard she moved on to the next room, where a boy

51

was patiently practicing Hanon. She sat down beside him and checked her watch: it was already after three; the phone call should have come at two. Perhaps Kayako had failed, as she'd thought. All the same, she wished she'd let her know quickly; being kept in such suspense was hard on the nerves. She considered calling her sister's place to find out, but, on second thoughts, there was nothing she could do if she did learn the result an hour or two sooner. If possible, too, she wanted to avoid talking to her sister until she knew.

The boy continued playing Hanon at his own pace. He seemed to be concentrating anxiously on the way he held his fingers. She couldn't remember what instructions she'd given him the week before, but she must have told him to strike the keys with the tips of his fingers and not bend them back.

Without comment, Kōko glanced through the window, which over-looked the spacious interior of the music store. Directly below was the record department, on the right stood rows of brass instruments, and the display window facing the main street held a white grand piano. Their own window wasn't there to be looked through from this side; the management had put in the glass to give a good view of them from all parts of the store and thus attract business for the school. Behind the bluish panes, Kōko and the children wriggled soundlessly like fish in an aquarium. When new to the job she was acutely aware of being watched and used to duck into the corridor just to yawn. She soon discovered, however, that hardly anyone was interested enough to stand and watch. At most the store manager might cast an eye occasionally over the row of five windows, close under the store's ceiling, to observe Kōko at work. Even then, unless she were gesticulating wildly, he would have difficul-ty making out her movements at this distance.

"Yes, that's a great improvement. Now try it again the same way, but a little faster this time. Like this: da-da-da-da-da."

Tensely, the boy tried to obey her instructions, promptly forgot his fingering, and scrambled the notes.

"No, wait!" Kōko cried in dismay. The boy tucked his head down and sneaked a glance at her face.

Just then there was a knock at the practice-room door. Kōko hurried to answer, calling in a high-pitched voice. Sure enough, she was wanted on the phone.

Kōko ran quickly to the office.

It was Kayako. Maybe she'd passed. Kōko sounded unexpectedly excited as she asked: "How did you get on? It was announced at one o'clock, wasn't it?"

Kayako's reply was muffled. She repeated her question louder: "How did you do?"

"Mm . . . no good. . . . " The sound of childish crying continued —perhaps it was easier to cry on the phone? Flustered, Kōko turned her back on the other people in the office, shielding the receiver. She was curiously disappointed at the news. If Kayako must take the exam, she had wanted her to pass (though actually enrolling at the school was another matter). Her grades hadn't been at fault, she was sure; then she thought suddenly of the copy of the family register that she'd fetched from the ward office for Kayako's application. Was that it? The thought was galling. In as level a voice as she could manage, she said:

"Oh dear, that's a pity. . . . But public schools have their good points too, you know. You mustn't take it too seriously. Exams are a matter of luck, not ability. . . . "

"But," Kayako burst out tearfully, "I can't go back to Auntie's. . . . I don't want to go back. . . . "

"Where are you now?"

". . . At home. It's in the usual mess. I nearly died. . . . "

"Now there's no need to talk like that! Anyway, it's a good thing you're there. I can be home about six, so why don't we eat out somewhere? Or else—Kayako, would you like to come and meet me here?"

"Mm."

"Well, then, come direct and stand in front of the window by the main entrance. Let's see—about five-thirty, okay?"

"Mm. . . . And, Mom, I haven't phoned Auntie yet."

"That's all right, I'll do it."

". . . I'm sorry."

Kōko winced as Kayako began to cry loudly again. "There's nothing to apologize about. Anyway, be here at five-thirty, will you?"

She hung up, but for a moment could not leave the phone.

"Anything wrong, Miss Mizuno?" It was the woman who did the general office work. She was fortyish, an old member of the staff, and unmarried. Though a pleasant enough person, she didn't seem well liked within the company. Kōko was unable to feel friendly toward her, either.

"My daughter. As they get bigger they come up with all sorts of new troubles, you know."

"I'm sure they do. You know, Miss Mizuno, you look like you've put on weight lately. I could be wrong, though?"

"I may have put on a little. Well, I must be getting back, I've left the children to their own devices. Thank you."

Between the office and the third-floor practice rooms, Kōko never took her eyes off her waistline. Was it noticeable already—in the third month? Did one get so big so soon? She'd put on another five pounds in the past week, till she tipped the scales at a hundred and twenty-two pounds; she'd gone to the public bathhouse the other day especially to weigh herself. Her wardrobe was gradually becoming unwearable. Since her day-to-day contacts were almost entirely with children, however, she hadn't been too concerned so far. The children didn't see their piano teacher as human, anyway.

So the question of Kayako had apparently resolved itself, one way or another, but what should she do about *this*? A forlorn anxiety stole over her. She was horrified by the changes that had actually begun to appear in her body. While she felt steadily worse, her appetite alone was growing heartier by the day. At this very moment, even as her chilly fingers and toes were starting to shiver and a sensation like frost in her veins crept through her body, she was so hungry that she scarcely knew what to do with herself; her mouth filled with saliva at the thought of where she'd take Kayako for the promised dinner.

As she walked along an empty corridor, she could no longer hold back the tears.

Reaching the practice rooms she was surrounded again by the sound of the children at their pianos; the same Beyer, Hanon, and Czerny.

On this particular day Kōko had the afternoon lessons. In that short space of time, twenty children passed through her hands. Teaching so many pupils should, in theory, have brought in a tidy sum, but the amount Kōko received monthly was barely enough to cover her own and Kayako's needs. She supposed she should consider herself lucky, as she had no diploma in music and the job was better than she deserved. She'd been teaching at the music store for three years now. Since the store offered lessons with its pianos as a kind of after-sale service, most of her pupils had never played a note in their young lives, and they came and went in a fast turnover. Kōko was able to hold down the job for these very reasons; yet once in a while she would have liked to hear the full tones of a piano well played.

As she was drilling a child on raising and lowering his forefingers, Kōko happened to think of Michiko, the friend who had found her this job, and how long it was—more than a year—since she'd seen her last. Perhaps she could go and ask her advice in a casual sort of way. Michiko was married but childless. No doubt she was still giving private piano lessons as energetically as ever. Michiko had put in a music room at home a couple of years ago, so that she could set up her own school. Kōko had received an invitation to her pupils' recital at the end of that year, and had taken Kayako with her to the concert hall.

She and Michiko had been taught from an early age by the same teacher. But Kōko had looked down on the piano as something that polite young ladies dabbled in; and while Michiko took her diploma in piano at a private conservatory, Kōko had been a literature major. She kept up her piano studies, though, from force of habit. Eventually her teacher arranged for her to take two pupils. Delighted to find that this paid far better than tutoring in the regular subjects, Kōko began to teach two little sisters in their home. And she'd relied on the piano for her living ever since.

And yet she had never thought that masquerading as a piano teacher might be the only thing she was good for; at least, not until after the divorce. Masquerade or not, she was coolly carrying it off—and collecting a good wage for her trouble. The knowledge even gave her a sense of superiority. But when she began to live alone with Kayako, Kōko was finally forced to admit how little she had to fall back on. Feeling utterly at a loss, she'd gone to beg a favor of Michiko, who was teaching at a piano school sponsored by a foundation. And Michiko went to considerable effort, even asking her own professor to lend his name, to find her this more secure job.

Kōko had Michiko to thank, then, for making it somehow possible to spend her days as she pleased; though, as she wasn't conscious of any great distance between them, she had never expressed her gratitude properly.

At the recital, a little over a year ago, Kōko had understood something for the first time: that in the end she had let everything slip away from her, that in reality she hadn't a single resource. It was an alarming discovery. Not only for her own sake—for she'd never made a genuine effort to teach Kayako the piano, either. What had she ever given Kayako? In fact, she was robbing her daughter of what she had while she persisted in living so erratically, so selfishly. When her mother was alive she had kept an eye on Kōko, but her mother had died six months earlier.

It was there, at Michiko's class concert, that Kōko put this thought into words: *I have nothing.*

Afterward, she had simply delivered her bouquet backstage and gone home. She hadn't seen Michiko since, not wanting another taste of the alarm that had filled her that day. Now, though, for the very same reason, Kōko needed to see Michiko. The fact that Michiko hadn't had a child of her own would be a great help, too. In her predicament, Kōko

56

wouldn't be spared Michiko's scorn for a moment. She made up her mind to phone, perhaps that evening.

Her last pupil for the day was a newcomer, a seven-year-old boy. His mother sat in a corner of the room, looking more tense than he did. The lesson Kōko gave was hardly a lesson at all. She told them which texts to buy at the sheet music counter, recommended several other books and records, and added a word about the right approach. The boy should be made to do the exercises daily, however briefly, and if possible one of his parents should keep him company. Politely, the mother began to talk about her son—how the boy's music-loving father had certain hopes for him, how she wanted him to develop his finer feelings as he matured, how he was a nervous child with few friends, and so on. Kōko smiled and nodded. Normally she would have made a beginning at once, teaching the boy to read music, but she was feeling too heavy and listless. While his mother talked the boy kept his forehead pressed to the window overlooking the store floor. His back view reminded Kōko irresistibly of the time—had Kayako been so small?—when she'd been seeing Doi frequently. They had often gone out as a threesome, Kayako, Doi, and herself, to department stores. In fact, they'd been to the one nearby.

On weekends when Doi stayed overnight, Kōko would be reluctant to let him go in the morning, to send him back to his family; and Doi, too, would hesitate, not wanting to get to his feet and go off alone, until by some sort of tacit agreement they would set out together with Kayako. Then they'd start wondering where to go. Since they'd come out for no good reason they seldom had anywhere in mind; they would have liked to stay quietly in the apartment. They sometimes went to zoos or amusement parks for Kayako's sake, but they couldn't do that every weekend.

Doi generally left the choice entirely up to Kōko. If she took too long to decide, he would say there was nowhere worth going in the city anyhow, and after a cup of coffee somewhere nearby he'd go off by himself, leaving Kōko overcome with remorse like a child who'd let a promised reward slip through her fingers. Afraid of making the same mistake again, the next time she would blurt out the name of some department store, though it might be the last place she wanted to go.

As long as Kōko had somewhere definite in mind, even if it took him out of his way, Doi would always head straight there. And department stores were certainly useful places for frittering time away. The rooftop playgrounds, mini-zoos, aquariums, gardens, and stage shows provided easy amusement, while browsing slowly through the displays of books, records, toys, and sports gear helped consume more time. Another regular stop was the food department in the basement. If they happened to find something special, some imported delicacy among the canned goods, Doi would buy one for Kōko; or sometimes he'd get two and take the other home.

They generally separated after lunch in the store cafeteria. Kōko and Kayako would give Doi a cheery send-off, for Kōko knew she couldn't press him to waste any more time. But this left her alone in the store with Kayako, and always at a loss: there was nothing to do there, nothing of interest; and yet she could never go straight home. Instead she would hustle Kayako along to a bargain sale of children's wear or to look at kitchen utensils.

Once, Doi had gone into a drugstore and asked for a particular nutritional supplement. Kōko wanted to know what it was. –Just something I was asked to pick up– he said. The clerk brought a package which Kōko recognized as a supplement for pregnant women. Laughing, she observed –So you're having another child, are you?– She was being sarcastic: surely Doi's wife couldn't be pregnant again after all that had happened?

–Yes– was the answer, –as a matter of fact we are. I don't suppose it bothers you, does it?–

Five months later Doi's second child was born.

Still staring at the boy's back, Kōko wondered whether that conversation, and others like it, had reached Kayako's ears too. By that time their department-store rambles with Doi had been going on for three years, and five-year-old Kayako had grown into a girl of eight. It was possible she remembered each scene more clearly than her mother did.

At the time it hadn't occurred to Kōko that Kayako had a memory. Far from it. Shortsightedly, she'd been convinced it was much better for Kayako to see her mother smiling with a man she loved (whatever their relationship might be in other people's eyes) than to see her lonely, tight-lipped, and grim. Lips without lipstick, set in a hard line: Kōko's own mother had been like that. Unlike her older sister, Kōko knew their mother only as a widow, a staunch protector of her children who had looked more than ten years older than she was. As a child, Kōko had feared and hated this mother who never relaxed her guard.

When 5:30 arrived Kōko sent the boy and his young mother home, after scheduling his next lesson, then hurriedly made ready to leave. She tidied and locked the five practice rooms and returned the keys to the office, where she also handed in her quota of attendance cards and clocked out. At 6:30 the evening teacher would come for the keys. Of the five regular teachers on the roster, Kōko taught for the smallest number of hours. The woman in the office called to her again: "Thanks for locking up. I wish I could leave with you, but I'm on the late shift today. What a drag! Why don't we go somewhere nice for a meal, sometime soon?"

"Yes, that's a good idea." As she spoke, Kōko asked herself whether deciding to have the baby would mean she'd have to quit this job.

"I wonder if I could put on as much weight as you, if I ate enough."

" . . . Do I really look so fat?"

"You're just right, now. You were too thin before."

"Really? It's not easy to tell, myself. . . . Well, if you'll excuse me, I must be going."

With a smile and a bow Kōko hurried from the office. The baby was really no reason to give up the job of her own accord; in fact, it would have been out of character for Kōko the charlatan to quit now. What she really wanted was to be made a full employee, because apart from raising her income this would entitle her to maternity leave, health insurance, and other benefits. No, why should she give it up?—but in practice she wasn't at all sure how much she could take if the going got rough. Kōko hadn't found friendship among the people she'd worked with for three years; instead, they had been very understanding, seeing her as a no-nonsense woman raising a daughter single-handed, and making allowances for her accordingly. No one ever complained when she was a little late for work or left a little early; it was accepted that she was hard-pressed.

Yes, she was forced to admit, if she was going to have the baby it would be much simpler to quit. Perhaps Michiko would find her another job: she knew it was a lot to expect, but she couldn't quite give up the idea.

Kayako was leaning against the big window where the white grand piano was on display, gazing up at an old building opposite. She was wearing the warm white sweater that Kōko had bought her after the interview ten days earlier. Her mouth hung half open, and she didn't notice Kōko at her side. Laying a hand on her head, Kōko said, "You'll turn into a goldfish if you stand there with a face like that."

"Oh, Mom," Kayako murmured, not much surprised. Kōko noted, with a sense of anticlimax, that the violent emotion she had shown over the phone was already under control. Kōko had imagined her clinging to her breast in tears, and had even been wary of Kayako's first move in case, in her own present state, she couldn't give her all the support she might need.

They went into a Chinese restaurant, Kayako's choice. At this hour they could expect a thirty-minute wait by the cloakroom before they were given a table. Kōko hardly knew the restaurant, but she had eaten there once, with Osada, the year before. She didn't remember what they'd talked about; all she remembered was the good fried shrimp with tōfu. (Sex always gave her a healthy appetite.) She intended to order the same thing today.

Kōko smiled at Kayako, who was gazing around curiously at the Chinese decor. "What are you looking so pop-eyed for? Anyone would think you'd never been in a place like this in your life."

Kayako dropped her eyes to the floor in confusion and answered in a small voice, "But it's true, I haven't."

"What? You've been lots of times. Have you forgotten?"

"I don't remember anything like this. . . . "

"We often ate at Chinese restaurants when you were in nursery school. Of course, they weren't so elegant. . . . But when your father was with us we went to even grander places than this."

That's funny, Kōko was thinking as she spoke, I'd completely forgotten about all that. Money, in Hatanaka's view, could always be expected to bubble up from somewhere. While Kōko was worrying and scrimping over their evening meal, he would turn up with money he'd blithely borrowed from someone or other to take her to an expensive restaurant. Even when they could no longer turn to Kōko's mother, Hatanaka never seemed to run short of people willing to lend. And although Kōko suspected that only a small fraction was ever repaid, that didn't seem to cost him anyone's friendship. Kōko didn't believe in borrowing money, and so, while Hatanaka's borrowings seemed like sleight of hand, she'd been too alarmed by his attitude to applaud these feats at the time. The fact that he wasn't deliberately setting out to defraud only made it worse.

Now, though, after nearly ten years, she was beginning to wonder: in the end, hadn't this fellow Hatanaka given her and Kayako more good times than anyone else? When had they ever had such a full life? This was certainly true of Kayako, anyway. But what did it mean? Was it a sign of how young they'd both been?—one thinking it was funny to take Kayako to fancy restaurants; and the other, unable to forget that the money they were spending wasn't their own, so irritated and ashamed that she wanted to run away.

Kōko felt a pang of nostalgia for the good times that had seemed to stretch as far as the eye could see. She was beginning to think that as long as they were having fun it made no difference how much irresponsibility was behind it.

61

"With Dad? Really?"

When they talked of her father, Kayako's voice would take on many shades—dazzled, and fearful, and embarrassed—all at once.

"Yes . . . to places we couldn't possibly go even now. It was crazy to eat there anyway, and crazier still to take a baby along, but we had so little money and your father had time on his hands, and so . . . we did it several times."

" . . . But wasn't he busy studying?"

"Hm, well. . . . "

Just then a waiter came to show them to a table. Kōko stood up briskly, grateful for his timing. She hadn't a hope of giving Kayako a true picture of those years. There they'd both been, partying irritably day after day, running through one unpayable loan after another. On days when they stayed home, company would turn up. They were both fleeing continually from the moment that would bring them face to face, alone together in their room.

Until Kayako was about nine, Kōko had explained her father's absence by saying simply that he'd gone somewhere far away. Kayako never asked expressly for details. Just after entering the fourth grade, however, she asked shamefacedly if she couldn't be allowed to see her father. After thinking it over till she was too weary to think further, Kōko contacted Osada and arranged for Hatanaka to have Kayako for a day, meeting her at a certain restaurant. From there, she heard afterward, they had gone to an amusement park where they licked frozen custards and watched an open-air show starring a children's TV hero.

The night before, as a precaution, Kōko had lightly told Kayako just one thing about the way her parents had parted: it had happened at a time that was very difficult for Dad because of all the studying he had to do. Hatanaka wasn't likely to talk about the circumstances either, unless he was questioned very closely.

It was true that Hatanaka had been struggling with examinations. She could account for the divorce that way if she wished, because he had set himself the sole duty of sitting at his desk until he passed the state law exam, making no attempt to earn an income in the meantime. But she was bewildered to find that now, nearly ten years later, she couldn't recognize any of the reasons—the debts, Hatanaka's lover, and the rest—that had once seemed as final as a blazing, consuming fire. Why *did* they get a divorce? They had simply been foolish and naive, that was all.

Now, when she sometimes talked with Kayako about her father, Kōko couldn't help seeing an accusation in the girl's veiled expression: why had she driven away such a kind and charming father? And she would very nearly let slip what was on her mind. You're right, she'd think, why did I, when we were having so much fun? The next moment, though, she'd be tempted to hide whatever might reflect badly on herself and deliver a stream of complaints about Kayako's father instead. She never could do that either, and in the end she would take guilty refuge in other subjects.

Kayako had asked to see her father barely three months after Kōko left Doi.

While Kayako was at the amusement park with Hatanaka, Kōko had walked the streets, cursing herself once more for not conceiving a child with Doi. Just one baby would surely have created so much that was new and different. She and Kayako were left behind, she realized, more alone than they had ever been. In the evening, at the agreed time, she went to meet Hatanaka and Kayako in the square outside the station. Noticing the relief on their faces when they saw her, she'd been struck by how very alone she and the child were.

When they were settled at the table and had given their order, Kayako finally began to discuss how she'd done in the exam. Outside the music store Kōko had thought she might be only barely in control of her distress, but she gave no sign of it, in fact she spoke quite easily.

"I wasn't really very confident from the start. Before the exam I kept having nightmares about failing."

Kōko tried for the same lighthearted tone as she protested, "What you were telling *me* sounded just bursting with confidence."

63

"You can't tell people you haven't any confidence in yourself."

Kōko laughed. "That's true. You can't let others see your weaknesses."

"No, you can't," Kayako agreed with such vehemence that Kōko had to laugh again.

"Well, it must be a relief to know finally, isn't it? What have you been doing?"

"Watching TV at home."

"Uh-huh. . . . "

"Did you ring Auntie for me?"

"Ah! I'd clean forgotten."

"After I asked you especially." Kayako's voice dropped instantly.

Kōko hastened to add: "She'll have guessed by now anyway, after not hearing for so long. . . . I can phone from home."

"But what if I get there before the phone call?"

"Get there? Get where?"

"Auntie's," was the muffled reply. As Kayako's voice grew fainter, Kōko's was getting louder.

"Auntie's? . . . You mean, you still intend to go back there? But you said you weren't going back again."

Kayako swelled out her cheeks in silence. She looked up at her mother from under her brows and rolled her eyes, indicating the tables to left and right as if to say "Look, you're making a scene in front of the other customers." This provoked more heated words from Kōko. Did the girl mean to suggest that Kōko was the one letting her emotions run away with her reason?

"And I thought that from today you were. . . . But since when can children come and go just as they please, eh? . . . You're just taking advantage of everyone's goodwill. You haven't a hope of getting into a cozy, snobby setup like that. They're a different race. . . . I've got a few thoughts on the subject myself, believe it or not. So you come right back where you belong."

Kōko broke off, her breath coming hard, and turned aside from

Kayako's flushed, glowering face. No, she couldn't keep it up, couldn't press her attack if Kayako decided to hurl her words back in her face. Wasn't it Kōko who had come and gone just as she pleased? Which of them had no idea how thoughtlessly she'd behaved? A few thoughts? She was afraid that Kayako would jab a finger at her and demand to hear what they were.

The food arrived. Kōko helped the waiter arrange the dishes on the table, giving him a pleasant smile. "This looks good, doesn't it?" she said encouragingly. "Take all you want, Kayako. . . . "

Kayako suddenly stood up. The tip of her nose was red.

"Why, what's the matter?"

Kayako looked down, dry-eyed, at her mother's face. Kōko looked back silently at her daughter's: a face that resembled her own, and Hatanaka's as well. How strange it was that one face could be the image of both parents. There was a kind of children's toy where the same picture turned out differently when held at different angles. Tilt it to the right and you saw her mother's face, to the left and you saw her father's, and yet full on you saw neither, but Kayako's own.

Kōko was frightened by Kayako's look. "The toilet?" she asked. Kayako shook her head blankly and opened her mouth. "I won't go back anywhere!" she cried and raced out of the restaurant. Kōko scrambled after her but lost her at once in the street; there were any number of places to hide if she chose. Kōko gave up hope of finding her and returned to the restaurant. When the waiter inquired what she wanted done about the meal, Kōko promptly decided to eat all she could; it would be a shame to let it go to waste. Kayako might wander around the streets for a little while, but sooner or later—when she got too hungry for one thing—she was sure to come home. But where? Kōko couldn't believe her daughter would come home to her. Far from being able to give the child what she was seeking, she was seeking the same thing herself.

When she had finished her meal, she went to the telephone at the cashier's desk and lifted the receiver. In the middle of dialing her sister's number she glanced up at the wall clock: it was 7:30. She pictured Kayako staring, mouth half-open, into the bright store windows of the downtown shopping district. It was still too early, she decided—Kayako would take a good hour to wander the streets. Now that she thought of it, the last time Kayako had been to Ginza after dark she would have been a mere infant, too young to remember. Kōko had the impression that she dragged her child around to all sorts of places for her own convenience, more so than other parents, but when she stopped to think about it she was sharply reminded how little Kayako knew of the world.

True, when Doi was there they had taken her out. Even so, they never went to the beach in the summer vacation, or on hiking trips. After Doi had gone, with Kayako already in the third grade, she tended to leave her in charge while she went out. When they did go out together, they mostly went shopping, and then only at a local supermarket. Before Kōko realized it the area around her home had become Kayako's whole world.

Kōko put the phone down and left the restaurant. She walked to the subway station and went straight home to the apartment. No Kayako. She lit the heater and washed a teapot and cup left in the sink—Kayako must have been drinking tea earlier in the day—then she called her sister's house. At the sound of Kōko's voice her sister almost snapped at the receiver.

"What on earth has happened to Kaya? She went to see the exam results and still isn't back."

Kōko automatically checked the clock on the refrigerator. Almost an hour had passed since she looked at the time in the Chinese restaurant.

"She should be back there very soon, I think. . . . " Kōko filled in what had happened, starting with Kayako's phone call during the day and ending with her bolting out of the restaurant.

"But why ever did she do that?"

"I'm not sure. She seems to have taken the failure very hard. . . . "

"Oh . . . goodness, do you think everything will be all right?"

"What do you mean?"

"As long as she comes home safely.... I wish she'd learn to under-stand that people are worrying about her."

"She understands, in her own way," Kōko retorted quickly. "I ap-preciate your concern for my daughter, but it's becoming more of a burden to her than a help."

She wanted to shout wildly—never mind whether it made any sense —*Kayako is mine!*

"What *are* you talking about? You'd better calm down a little. Kaya is bound to be all right. She's a good deal more sensible than you. Listen, why don't you come over and wait for Kaya here? How about it? I'd feel happier, too, if you were with us...."

"No, I have to wait for her here, she was talking about coming back home soon, for good."

"What?... But that's nonsense."

"Why? Why is it nonsense?"

"Oh, surely you realize...."

Shōko's voice was relaxed. Kōko remembered how her sister had laughed at her once for crying over something—when she was in junior high, perhaps? She'd been sad because a pet dog had taken sick and died, and her sister had said –Silly! What's all the fuss about?– She realized that she'd only wear herself out if she lashed out now; her blows would fall on thin air. Her sister's voice sounded undaunted.

"Anyway," Kōko said, "if she turns up, would you tell her, please, to contact me at once? I'll be waiting here."

"Of course I'll tell her, but ... I hope this makes you think about what's best for Kayako for a change. Kaya's lonely. She's got no father, and *you* care more about your own feelings than Kaya's. There may be nothing wrong at present, but what if she really takes to brooding some day, what if she even goes and kills herself? Give it some careful thought, once more, will you? Come to us, both of you. We've got your rooms waiting. I can just see how thrilled Kaya would be."

"... Thanks. I'm sorry to have worried you."

Kōko put the phone down. She looked at the clock again: it was four or five minutes before nine. She tried to remember what she'd said in the Chinese restaurant. What was she in the middle of saying? She remembered her disappointment when Kayako announced she wasn't coming back with her—her own mother. Confident that Kayako was returning home at last, she'd been reviewing the situation quite seriously: now that that's settled, she was thinking, what should I do next? First, she had decided, I'll have to go and collect Kayako's belongings.

The curtains were still open. She closed those in her own room, then crossed to Kayako's. She could see neon lights in the main street: signs advertising a sewing machine, a hotel, a confectioner's, a coffee shop, a sauna; too many to count. They should have sparkled brightly, but most of the view from the seventh floor was of dark sky, and perhaps this made the dots of light seem so poignant. They were like a luminescent moss clinging feebly to life in the depths of a marsh.

This is what Kayako looked out on night after night, she thought. Her gaze returned to the room itself. Lying on the desk was a small, worn pair of scissors that Kōko had bought her before she started school. Kayako's clever hands had made all kinds of things with them: a rabbit mask, dolls, a mouse in a suit of clothes. She was always busy with one project or another.

Kōko sat down at the desk and went back to watching the neon lights through the window. She wanted to hear Kayako's voice; but to her horror she could do nothing but wait. She had no idea what might happen next. This time Kayako might have gone for good. In the same breath she was fretting over what to say to the girl when she phoned from her aunt's house—as she might at any moment—and flinching as she felt Kayako's very being slip further and further from her touch. She had no concrete terms such as "death" or "runaway" in mind. It was simply that when she closed her eyes she could see Kayako's body being swallowed up, out of her sight, into a mass of people.

Once, after she began seeing Doi again, she had a dream in which she left Kayako with a total stranger to go on a journey with a boy, a fourteen- or fifteen-year-old who seemed almost like a girl. The two of them rode a bus along a mountain road. There were no other passengers. At the boy's insistence they got off, though they weren't at the end of the line, they were in the middle of nowhere. There was only the road, the mountainside, and the glowing evening sky. Kōko stood at the cliff's edge and gazed toward the setting sun. She felt a numbing loneliness. The boy spoke at her side. –What are you doing here?–

The sound of his voice brought Kōko to her senses: if she didn't go and pick up Kayako before it got dark she would never see her again; but she couldn't reach the town from there before the dead of night, no matter how fast she traveled.

In an unknown town, someone—she didn't know who—had said to her: –It's all right, I'll look after your child. We'll be waiting here, at the same place, around six o'clock.– The speaker had seemed kind, and so, against her better judgment, she'd gone off leaving Kayako behind. The same place, at six o'clock: it was her one remaining link with Kayako. But she couldn't make it in time. She had no way of getting in touch, either, since she didn't know who the person was. She would never see Kayako again. Kōko began to tremble. Kayako was growing more distant now with every moment. Why had she ever let go of her hand?

The boy asked: –What's wrong? Aren't you going to sketch?– Kōko had a large sketchbook under her arm.

–But . . . my child. . . . – Kōko swallowed the words she'd been about to say. It was too late. Already, she had no child.

–Child? What child?–

–It doesn't matter.–

Shaking her head tearfully, Kōko opened her sketchbook. She had to admit it was a beautiful rose-colored sunset.

When she awoke, Kōko had been afraid all over again. She knew the self whose image she'd just seen, the woman poised for flight, ready to dump her child and set off with the boy alone; for that had been her real self, wanting to recapture the time she'd had alone with Doi when they were students. It made an ugly sight: a mother who cursed her child's existence. And it seemed pure luck that she had kept afloat so far without seeing Kayako sink out of sight.

There was that time when Hatanaka took three-year-old Kayako away to his home town and didn't return for over a week.

And the time when Kayako was one, and running a high temperature, with an ear infection after measles.

Once she began to remember, it seemed she'd always been haunted by the fear of having Kayako taken from her. For all her usual irresponsibility—or maybe because of it—the slightest thing would bring on an anxiety that darkened her whole outlook: I won't be allowed to raise a child safely, after all. With Kayako's feverish body like an overcooked carrot in her arms, she'd felt too weak to get her to a doctor.

It was past ten o'clock when the phone rang at last in Kōko's apartment. Kayako had wandered about the shopping arcades in the station building and then made one complete circuit on the Yamanote Line before going home. Kōko said only: "Apologize properly to Auntie for all the worry you've caused her," and hung up. Kayako's voice was so unchanged that it made Kōko's head swim. It was as if nothing had ever happened. She was exactly the same Kayako as before. If Kōko could actually have seen her she might have been able to accept this with thankful relief; but a reunion with only the sound of her voice left her uneasy, as if it might have been some sort of trick.

After several drinks, Kōko got up toward midnight and headed for the phone. She dialed Michiko's number. She wanted to tell her what she planned to do, and hear her say in turn, "You must be out of your mind, get an abortion straight away." Michiko was the kind of person who might go with her, might drag her all the way to a clinic. Kōko was afraid that unless she could be deflected by some external force she'd just go right ahead and have the baby.

The ringing signal continued until, on the fifth ring, she hung up. Then, reeling from the alcohol, she turned off the kitchen light and heater and went into her room.

She changed into a nightgown and, lying down at last, was seized immediately with nausea. She bent over the washbasin, tears springing to her eyes. In her drunken wretchedness, Kōko forgot all that had happened that day.

4

Kōko was on a boat. A tightly sealed little ark. Thick glass panes were set into the ceiling and portholes, the passengers were so crowded together they could barely move, and the air was hot and close. Kōko was staring at the deep red that spread away beyond the fogged panes. It was dark on board, almost too dark to distinguish faces. She wasn't sure whether there was someone with her on the boat; if there was, perhaps it was some stranger she'd just met on board. Or it might be someone she'd promised many, many years ago to meet there. And yet she didn't remember any such promise, nor could she think who it might be.

Being on the boat felt exactly like being in a town where she'd once lived: at any moment she expected—nervously, but wistfully, too—to meet someone who recognized her. Then when she steeled herself to look over the crowd once more, there was nobody she knew.

Outside the portholes stretched the crimson twilit sea. The horizon made long sweeps like the needle of an instrument. The water that lay ahead was suffused with a deeper red. The sleekly undulating surface continued its vast, endlessly recurring motion, its shores long since forgotten. Was there a storm? The vessel was riding the waves up and down, dipping and rising, like an elevator, and all at sixty miles an hour. Kōko was surprised to hear this murmured among the other passengers—could she really be inside something traveling at that speed? —for the sea appeared almost unchanging, neither merging with the dusk nor flaring more brilliantly red. There was no sign of land. Just think how vast the sea must be, Kōko told herself as she stared steadily out of the window. . . .

Kōko had this dream in early April. The color of the sea and the lurching of the boat stayed with her for some time afterward.

She was still puzzled by that obscure feeling about the passengers in the dream: who *was* it she'd expected to find there with her? Doi seemed the most natural answer, but surely if he'd been there he would have shown up clearly. She'd never gone anywhere by boat with Doi, though they had once looked at a travel poster for a hovercraft that could do sixty miles an hour.

Try as she might, she couldn't identify her companion. Though this was only to be expected of a dream, Kōko wasn't satisfied. Before she'd finished she even began to fancy that the man's baby had been in her arms. She was sure she'd been holding something warm and breathing.

April was the fifth month since Kōko's fetus first drew breath. By now she could no longer hope to hide the bulge. Not only was her belly swelling, but she was so fat she'd developed a double chin. Of course she'd put on weight with Kayako, too, but nothing like this. She thought there might be something wrong, but she had yet to see a doctor. She continued to put it off—even with the fetus stirring faintly now. The thought of having the baby was terrifying, but the thought of an abortion was more wretched than she could bear. To choose to give birth at least offered a release from facing such wretchedness directly.

She had only seen Kayako once since the day the exam results were announced. Kayako had told her over the phone that she wanted to stay a while longer at her aunt's. She was going to join the family on their spring trip to Nara, and planned to get in some piano lessons as well during the vacation.

Kōko asked when school was due to start, and reluctantly allowed her to stay until it did. Immediately afterward, she enrolled Kayako at the local junior high—where they'd agreed she was to go—and bought a school satchel and regulation clothing, which she told Kayako to come and pick up. For a treat she had a shortcake ready: the sight of it on the table raised the only smile to be seen from Kayako that day. It was a special favorite of hers that Kōko bought twice a year, on her birthday and at Christmas.

Kayako departed quickly, however, without touching on what Kōko was waiting to hear. Kōko stuck to the subject of getting ready for school, and Kayako seemed so ill at ease she didn't try too hard to keep her.

She hadn't seen Kayako since. In the month that had passed, the bulge had grown distinctly bigger. There was nothing for it but to tell her, the next time they met, about her mother's untimely pregnancy. Kōko expected this would be on the day the school opened, the tenth of April. She did want to go to the opening ceremony, for Kayako's sake. And it was only days away.

She continued her daily round at the music store. In the past she would have been afraid to show herself; she might have taken to her heels and hidden; whereas now (and this made her aware of her age) she went to work out of force of habit and got away with it, though only just, blunting speculation with evasions and pretense. The sheer effrontery of it made her blush. At twenty she'd had an abortion, without a moment's hesitation, solely because she feared for her reputation. There had hardly been any concrete reasons against her having the baby: she would probably have carried it off a good deal more gracefully than she could now. Doi would have been aghast—he was almost as young as Kōko—but ultimately he'd have stood by her and the baby. He would have grumbled at the mess she'd landed them in, but he might have registered a legal marriage with Kōko, also for appearances' sake. As a student he'd been timid and sensible enough to do that, and Kōko, on her side, wouldn't have dared take advantage of his timidity. In fact, she had never even thought that she might one day have a child. She had found the idea uncanny, almost unimaginable.

At this point, no one who worked with Kōko had linked her size with pregnancy. They were all worried about her, suggesting something might be wrong, that it might be a sign of some malignant disease. Not even the woman in the office suspected the truth.

"It can't be healthy, whichever way you look at it. Take your hands; look how the veins stand out. It's tiredness catching up with you, if you ask me."

Whenever people talked like this, Kōko would appear concerned for a moment or two, then laugh it off. "Oh, it must be the menopause, it's that time of life."

This would make them laugh, and for the time being they'd take their eyes off her body. Kōko would feel a moment's scorn—they were so blind, the lot of them. Later, when she was alone, she was always disgusted with herself: what an idiotic reason to feel superior!

Nevertheless, there was a limit to how long she could hide her pregnancy at work, and time was running out.

Every night Kōko would resolve: I'll do it tomorrow. I'll have Kayako come, I'll tell her about my condition, and I won't give her a chance to catch her breath this time. I'll tell her to leave her aunt's house and come back to her mother. By the next morning, though, she'd be reluctant to stir up such a fuss; anyway, she hadn't entirely made up her mind yet. And she would drift through another day like all the others.

The day before Kayako's school ceremony, however, her sister phoned. Would she mind coming over later, because she had something special to discuss? "Well," Kōko replied, "it'll have to be in the evening, but yes, I will come. There's something I've been wanting to talk about, too."

When she put down the receiver, Kōko's legs started to shake. She could see how it would turn out now: one thing would quickly lead to another, and she'd end up having the baby. Kōko wasn't sure if she was pleased or frightened that things had been set in motion so casually. The dark red sea of her dream floated up at eye level. Its surface heaved. Kōko closed her eyes. Sixty mph . . . 120 mph. The boat. The boat was flying through the air. It wouldn't stop. Nobody would stop it. The surge of acceleration almost whirled her bodily away. She wanted to be sick.

She groped to a chair at the table, sat down, and opened her eyes. The red curtains in Kayako's room were swaying. Outside the open window spread a soft, white, overcast sky. From the kitchen she could see nothing but sky.

She had just finished breakfast, and an uneaten crust and a coffee cup were still on the table. The bread crumbs had sopped up some splashes of coffee. Kōko started slowly wiping them up. There was nothing she need fear. Nothing. She continued stubbornly rubbing the table top, as if inscribing words with the cloth.

Her sister couldn't stop her either. She would be appalled, and might finally turn her back on her, but that was all. And what if Kayako did come home? That wouldn't get her out of this foolish business of the baby. Freedom. There was nothing to prevent her doing whatever she pleased, because she *had* nothing. Nothing. She used to think that simply being Kayako's mother gave her life a solid social value; but had it really counted for anything? Here she was, the same mother, with this great distended belly and the wild idea of actually having the baby, and yet no sentence of death had been passed on her. No stones fell from heaven, nobody came after her brandishing a gun, though she rather hoped they would. Of course not: with no proper job, no husband, nothing, she could do what she liked and it wouldn't matter. Freedom. A fine estate. Kōko clenched the dishcloth in her hands. Yes, that's what she was afraid of. No one would have anything to say; not any more. She thought longingly of her mother who used to drag her by the arm and sit her, screaming and wailing, at the piano till she did her lesson.

Kōko dropped the cloth, got up, and went into her room, where she stood before the mirror and studied her body: the front, the right side, the left. She smoothed down her skirt to check the line of her abdomen. Too swollen for five months. No choice of clothes would disguise it. She couldn't recall what she'd been like when she was expecting Kayako and so couldn't compare her size now, but something told her that the baby was growing too big. Maybe, since her routine provided so little exercise, the baby was getting fat and lazy like its mother. It didn't move much; Kayako, although a girl, had moved a lot.

Kōko stared at her legs and face. Look at those rolls of flesh—not a trace of youth anywhere. An ugly, fat woman. She simply couldn't bring herself to look at her bare stomach. If I were having this baby with Doi, she thought, I needn't have grown so ugly. How faithful the body is to the spirit.

Kōko moved back to the kitchen and turned on the television. She still had an hour to spare before leaving for work. She put the kettle on again and had a cup of instant coffee while she watched a puppet show. Even now, that sort of program made her absentmindedly want to call Kayako to come and watch. Until just four or five years ago, Kayako was always in front of the set, open-mouthed, too absorbed to hear Kōko speak till her arm or shoulder was jogged. Then she'd look up trembling at her mother's face and set about her chores: there were dishes to be washed, or her help was wanted with the cooking.

Kōko suddenly got up and snapped off the TV. She hurriedly made ready and left the apartment. There was no one else in the elevator. It was not too late yet. Hurry, she told herself, as she broke into a run down the road to the station. But she lost her breath at once and her legs refused to move forward under the weight of her body. How could she have let herself get into this shape, she wondered, coming to a standstill at the curb and searching for a taxi. She wanted to rush to a clinic—any one would do—and have her womb emptied before going to get Kayako back. At this late stage it might involve more than just a simple procedure; she might have to be admitted to the hospital. Even so, there was still time. Though she wouldn't be able to attend Kayako's school opening, she could meet her a week later as the same mother she had always been. She didn't know what to do for Kayako after that. But there must be something she could do.

She had missed the prize-giving at the elementary school, too. She'd been waiting to hear from Kayako, but in the end the girl must have gone alone. What was done was done, however: from now on Kayako would need her mother.

Kōko was ready to stamp her feet in frustration before she finally got hold of a taxi. She quickly gave the driver the name of a Yamanote Line station, chosen at random—it was an area she didn't know—and no sooner had the automatic door swung shut than she was begging him to go as fast as he could. There was no time.

She knew it was a spur-of-the-moment decision. If she started to think about it in a calmer frame of mind, she would probably come to her senses, realizing how foolish she was being, and get out of the taxi on the spot. What she was doing amounted to a denial of everything she'd ever done: clinging to Doi at the expense of Kayako; keeping Hatanaka away from Kayako; choosing not to go home to her mother with Kayako; everything.

She could hear her sister's voice now, drawing gradually closer: so you've finally begun to understand what a bad mother you've been, how little sense you've shown? And hear herself protest: no, that's not it—don't think I've liked choosing a different world from other people. I know I've been stubborn—but not about Kayako alone. All my life, though often I haven't known which way to turn, I *have* managed to make choices of my own. I don't know if they were right or wrong. I don't think anyone can say that.

One thing, though, was certain: that she had never betrayed the small child she'd once been; the child who had pined for her brother in his home for the retarded; the child who had watched her mother and sister resentfully, unable to understand what made them find fault with her grades, her manners, her language. And she was not betraying that child now, thirty years later. This, she had always suspected, was the one thing that mattered. And although she was often tempted by a growing awareness of the "proper thing to do" once Kayako was born—not only in the harsh advice she was constantly offered by others, but within her

78

own mind—in the long run her choices had always remained true to her childhood self.

But now, just for the moment, she wanted to find an answer to this problem and be done with it—to let sheer momentum carry her there. She was on the way to a featureless but comfortable place known as "common sense." She was well aware, though, that if the taxi didn't get her there soon she would remember her childhood again, remember how she'd tagged along after her brother, and turn the taxi around. Hurry, hurry, she thought, more and more frantically. The driver seemed to be saying something, she didn't know what.

When she was set down in front of an unfamiliar inner-city station, there was a slight movement in her womb. Kōko pressed her hand firmly over her abdomen as she watched the yellow taxi drive away. It was soft: her hand sank deeper and deeper into the soft flesh. Flesh, and then a small enclosed sea. What must it be feeling, floating on this sea of darkness? Kōko tried to listen to the fetus's voice. She couldn't hear anything, she could only sense the breathing of something there, already clinging to its mother.

People were streaming in and out of the station. The wind was warm and damp. Traffic signals blinked, and an electric signboard registered the noise level. These were the only spots of brightness; there were no shadows on the ground. It was a monotonous, inorganic scene, like Hanon played by a small child, the notes all disconnected. Kōko started walking. On the back streets there were sure to be two or three clinics that would perform an abortion unconditionally. She had looked for a doctor in the same way as a student, though in a different part of the city. Nearly twenty years ago. Kōko walked on, staring at the ground beneath her feet. The pale, dry sidewalk looked like the shallows of a river, its flow broken here and there by tiny eddies. Glistening spray was flung up around people's feet. A child's pink sandals approached and moved away. A coffee shop's Coca Cola sign on a stand came up and bumped her. Kōko carefully set it straight before walking on. Though it was only early April, she was beginning to sweat as she walked.

Three big plastic buckets had been set out to dry in a row, upside down. A scrubbing brush was drying beside them. Walking with her eyes on the buckets, Kōko caught her foot on the first. All three tumbled over noisily, one by one. Flustered, Kōko gave chase as they rolled onto the roadway. Horns blared around her. Kōko ignored the impatient traffic while she gathered the buckets together. As she did so, the word "illusion" echoed in her ears. Illusion. Were the road, the cars, the buildings, the sky, all an illusion? Was she, too, merely floating like a scrap of thread through an illusory universe?

Only two buckets had rolled all the way onto the road. Kōko returned to the sidewalk with the pair in her hands. A woman in a cook's apron was waiting intently beside the third.

"I'm so sorry, you shouldn't have bothered, and in your condition too—you did give me a turn! What's a plastic bucket when you've got the baby to think of? Take care, won't you? . . . "

Kōko handed the woman the buckets she'd retrieved, bowed, and hurried away. She was hot. Terribly hot. Kōko stopped and laid her hands over her stomach. Its round mass felt ready to blaze up, spurting flames, at any moment. What she had there was no longer her own belly, to do with as she pleased, so how could she spread her thighs and have someone lay hands on the hot living thing inside? She remembered the word "sin" with a cold shudder. The clammy vinyl surface of the delivery table. The nurse's expressionless face as she positioned the light. The clinking of metal instruments. The stained floor tiles. The sound of the doctor's leather scuffs. As she left the recovery room the nurse had told her she'd been screaming for another injection, quick, quick, in a near frenzy as she came out of the anesthetic. She didn't remember. All she remembered was a sickening rush of blurred sensations as though her body were slithering down into the abyss of death.

She had had that abortion before she could see the delivery table as a place where babies were born. And then, on a similar table in another hospital, she had given birth to a baby. The baby was Kayako, and

Kayako was living still. She hadn't killed her, and now she couldn't lie on a delivery table for another abortion. She could see the baby all too well, its cells proliferating steadily toward only one end, the day of its birth. She couldn't kill it. When next she lay down on a delivery table it could only be to give birth. Biting her lip, Kōko looked around her.

She was quite late getting to the music store. Once again Beyer and Hanon began to filter back and forth.

Kōko's thoughts turned to the day her brother came home from the institution. He was ten years old. Dormitory life was so ingrained in him, he couldn't have his routine upset in any way: he had to wake at the proper time, wash his face, do morning exercises by the radio, then eat breakfast. And Kōko, who till then had been whiling away long solitary days of boredom—being too young for her sister—suddenly had the same regular habits thrust upon her.

Every morning, when their mother shrilled the order to rise, Kōko and her brother bounded out of bed and made a race of dressing and folding their bedding away. Their mother could hardly have been pleased that he needed this sort of treatment before he could function at all, but Kōko was delighted with the life they led after his return. She was sure there could be no happiness for her without her brother. For the first time, Kōko knew a kind of joy that had nothing to do with the intellect. The boy's emotions were unclouded: what pleased him meant joy, what displeased him meant anger; but he experienced his deepest joy in enduring what displeased him for the sake of those he loved. She wondered why. Though he lacked intelligence, he was endowed with love, which was another kind of wisdom. Kōko had been disappointed to realize that Kayako at the age of one already possessed more of the wits she needed to protect herself than her brother had at the age of ten; she was simply a miniature version of the adults who would calmly abandon one another for the sake of their own happiness. Kōko's pleasure was mixed as she watched Kayako display more intelligence each day.

Sometimes, when he couldn't make himself understood, her brother would fly into a rage, toppling furniture or swinging a baseball bat. But for his little sister Kōko he had nothing but smiles. When they raced into their clothes he always let her win; he would smile his approval, then hurry to put on his own. To him she remained a baby, a newcomer who could never do or understand a thing, and for all her admiration Kōko sometimes resented this from one who couldn't even talk properly himself; but it was nice, after all, to be indulged. It seemed that having a younger sister bolstered her brother's confidence in himself as a boy.

It was cold the day her brother came home. Their mother left the house early in the morning to go and collect him. Kōko waited with her sister in the living room, all day long. Shōko, in junior high school by that time, was reading a book. Kōko had few recollections of her sister ever playing with her. She barely spoke to Kōko that day, while Kōko grew cross with no way to occupy the hours. The thought of a life shared with her brother took her breath away and—more from dread than anticipation—she just couldn't hold still. She would start to talk and be scolded by her sister; she would wander about the living room and be scolded again.

She remembered her sister saying –If you're going to make a noise, why don't you go into the garden?– Normally she would have done as she was told, in spite of the cold, and played with the dog, but on this particular day she didn't want to leave her sister's side.

She couldn't remember what else they did until the others came home. In fact, she'd forgotten the homecoming itself. Perhaps, worn out by waiting, she had fallen asleep. In the morning, though, began the dazzling sunlit life of what her brother called "the mountain school." She studied with her brother, rode double on his bicycle in the yard, even went to the toilet when he did. Once their mother had caught them there comparing their efforts. They would also get lost together, and the name tag around her brother's neck proved useful then.

Then a cold her brother caught had turned into pneumonia, and he had died. He was Kayako's age. Kōko went back to being a quiet child, slow-moving about the house. When set to practice the piano she would go through the motions so mechanically that she spent a year on one gavotte; her sister, meanwhile, performed a piano solo at her school concert, much to their mother's delight.

Kayako answered the door. Kōko stood there tensely, trying to follow the change in her expression. Kayako was wearing a fluffy pink cardigan, probably another hand-me-down from Miho; she seemed to have settled very cozily into her aunt's home. Her eyes widened in initial surprise, then dropped awkwardly as she said in a small voice, "Come in. . . . I hardly recognized you. How did you get so fat?"

"It's not all fat," Kōko answered, smiling, as she took off her shoes. Kayako gave a halfhearted smile. Most likely she had taken it, without understanding, for some kind of joke. Kōko put on the slippers that Kayako set out for her and bent down to arrange her shoes neatly. Her swollen belly was uncomfortable, and she straightened up gasping for breath.

This was her first visit to the house since her mother's funeral, two years before, but very little had changed. The hall was brightly lit by a new chandelier, and the familiar watercolor of daffodils had been replaced by a modern woodblock print. The bronze vase had been replaced, too, by a glass horse.

Her sister and Miho were sitting on the living-room sofa watching television. They rose together when Kayako and Kōko entered.

"You've kept us waiting so long, we're all starving. Good gracious . . . what's happened? . . . You've got so fat."

Kōko could see Kayako slipping away to the kitchen. As her tall, slim back vanished from sight, Kōko answered, as nonchalantly as she could, "I'm sorry I haven't been to see you before, while you've been looking after Kayako."

"Yes, I should think so. I don't know what you've got against us, never dropping in even for a chat. You were always a funny stubborn old thing, though, so it's not surprising. But when did you get so fat? I hardly know who I'm talking to."

Miho looked up, glanced from her mother to Kōko, and said, "When I saw you a while ago, you weren't any different, were you, Aunt Kōko?"

Kōko nodded a greeting. "Ah, yes, it's a good school, isn't it? I'm awfully sorry about Kayako, after all the trouble you've gone to. Still, these things can't be helped, can they?"

"Actually, that's what I wanted to discuss with you," said her sister, half-rising to her feet, "and that's why I've asked you to come. But let's have dinner first. We mustn't keep the children waiting any longer. Papa will be a little late home from the office. Miho, dear, go and call your brother."

Miho answered brightly and went upstairs. Kōko felt a sudden wave of nostalgia as she wondered which of the upstairs rooms was now Takashi's. There were two rooms: her sister used to have the larger one and Kōko the smaller, facing east, but only after she reached junior high; until then she'd slept beside her mother in the room downstairs, with her brother alongside when he was at home. Now the downstairs bedroom had been redecorated in a Western style for Shōko and her husband. Kōko's old room upstairs looked out on the trees at a nearby shrine, and from her last year in school she had often watched the midsummer sun climb beyond the grove, and listened raptly to the crescendo of birds and cicadas as the sky brightened. Those skies were tinged with the most brilliant, refreshing colors of any dawn that Kōko had seen.

When Kōko and the others were seated, Kayako carried in a large tray of soup bowls. She kept her eyes lowered—embarrassed perhaps by her mother's presence—even while she was passing out the bowls. The maid, a slight girl whom Kōko hadn't seen before, also emerged from the kitchen to place a salad bowl and a set of dishes in the center of the table.

"Kaya, leave the serving to Misa and sit down, dear. Kaya's always like this, though I keep telling her she needn't bother. You've got her very well trained, poor girl."

Kōko forced a smile as she glanced at Kayako's red face. The girl was embarrassed, certainly, but above all she seemed tense about the coming discussion. And she wasn't the only one. Everyone was so preoccupied with what the day might hold that Kōko's fat stomach had passed for just that: fat. Kōko was disappointed. She'd been sure that the instant she set foot in her sister's house, exposing her shape to general view, there'd be pandemonium. She had thought out what to say in that case, but now she would have to formally announce that she was pregnant. How should she put it? She hadn't rehearsed anything suitably inane. Kōko cast her eye around the table till it came to rest on her high school nephew: surely *he* would notice? But he sat drinking his soup, looking unconcerned.

The meal progressed, and the expected scene still hadn't occurred. Her sister, in a good mood, described how they were finally going to rebuild next year, though her husband wasn't keen, preferring to spend the money, if it had to be spent, on enlarging his office; but her mind was made up, and she'd insisted that they rebuild the house next.

"I mean, it's served its time, hasn't it? We've made a lot of improvements over the years, but the actual foundations are nearly forty years old. I hate to think of the state they're in. And with these high ceilings it's cold, and dark too. . . . "

"Yes, the ceilings are very high."

"A good apartment like yours is the best answer—you don't have to worry. You may turn out to have done better for yourself than anyone else, before you're finished."

"Oh, no, not me. . . . Some people fall on their feet, others don't, and there's nothing we can do about it. . . . But you're always so amazingly active. Every time I hear from Kayako that you took her to a concert, or went cycling on your holiday or something, I do admire you."

Her sister exchanged smiling glances with her own children for a long moment, then suddenly grew serious. "But isn't there something wrong with you? They say that when your weight changes very quickly it generally means you're ill. It's awful, the amount you've put on. Have you been to a doctor?"

Kōko shook her head, unable to find her voice. It wasn't time yet, not

85

until dinner was over—or so at least she consoled herself. Not only had she lost her voice, but she was beginning to feel hot under the gaze of the three children. Strange, she thought, are people really so vague about what they see in others? Passengers on a train would surely be better judges of this bulging belly. Why were her sister and the children so very certain that she couldn't be pregnant? The unsuspecting looks on all their faces left her helplessly irritated—though she told herself she was behaving like a child who digs a trap and then feels thwarted when no one falls in.

Swallowing a mouthful of pork, her sister went on worrying about Kōko's health. "You'd better see a doctor, tomorrow if you can. Not a local man, mind—go to a university hospital. The others all blame everything on a cold. How much do you weigh now, for heaven's sake? You must be over a hundred and thirty pounds."

". . . I haven't weighed myself lately."

"You really are irresponsible, you know. Have you ever considered what would happen if you just dropped dead? I'm always worried about the possibility, myself. Though you mightn't think so to look at them, these children can't do a thing for themselves yet. . . . "

Miho blinked her round eyes, which were just like her father's, and put in: "Papa was told he had high blood pressure the other day, wasn't he?"

"That's right." Shōko seemed to enjoy this subject. "Papa has put on a lot of weight lately, like you, and we were all teasing him. So he went for a checkup, because, as he said, it's best to be on the safe side. Well, there was nothing seriously wrong, but they found he had high blood pressure. The doctor said that if he'd gone on straining himself the way he's been doing without knowing it, he mightn't be alive this time next year. That sent chills down our spines. Take my advice—you won't regret it. Even I go twice a year, though I've had no problems yet."

"My mother isn't ill. She drinks too much." Kayako lifted her head abruptly and spoke up. "She's always drinking, and leaving the place in a mess."

Kōko's eyes met her sister's, and she burst out laughing. The laughter, reverberating under the high ceiling, sounded unnecessarily loud.

"That's what's called a bombshell! Don't startle us like that!"

"But, you know, it just might be true," Shōko said brightly. "You should be glad you've got such a sensible daughter. There's a lot of her grandmother in her."

Takashi asked permission to leave the table and walked off. When she saw this nephew of hers on his feet Kōko was amazed at how he'd grown. If only his features were a little firmer, she thought idly, he'd be the ideal teenager. Did he remember his aunt carrying him as a baby to see the trains and play in the park? He'd been a nervous, timid child. He was the first baby born to someone close to Kōko. By the time Miho was born, Kōko was living with Hatanaka, and she barely remembered her arrival at all.

Miho and Kayako followed him away from the table and sat down in front of the TV. Her sister, she found, had already finished her meal and was sipping tea. Kōko hurried to finish the meat on her plate. Her sister had moved on to the subject of where to send Takashi to college: he hadn't a chance of getting into a national university in any case, she said, so instead of doing a second-rate degree in law or economics (which he wouldn't be interested in, anyway) he might as well study design or architecture or something of the sort, but the boy wasn't clear in his own mind yet, so they didn't know what to do. The more they thought about it, the harder it was to decide.

When she saw that Kōko was finished, Shōko stood up and tried to hurry her away: "Look, we shouldn't really talk in front of the children, so let's go into the sitting room."

Kōko was about to nod, but she hastily shook her head instead. Kayako was staring at her mother. Diffident, confused eyes. Kōko thought of the girl's father and how often she'd encountered those same eyes; she'd been puzzled to see him so apprehensive, so anxious-looking. Her earliest impressions of Hatanaka and her image once they lived apart had been reduced to those hollow eyes. And yet surely, in fact, Hatanaka had always been inflated with his own importance.

87

"I'd rather stay here. The children are old enough to listen, they won't mind."

"But we can't be comfortable here, and. . . . "

"I'll listen to whatever you want to say here."

"Oh, no, that won't do. Come along."

"But it's about Kayako, isn't it? In that case I want to know the children's feelings, too. . . . "

Her sister, still on her feet, looked over at the big children in front of the TV set, gave a sigh, and took her seat again at the dining table.

"You haven't changed, have you?" she said.

"I'm sorry. . . . It's just that I'd like Kayako to be here too, if you're going to talk about her, and I've also got something to tell you all. . . . "

Kōko spoke apologetically. The maid was unhurriedly clearing the table. Kōko had a feeling that she'd been having the same kind of argument with her sister, and her mother too, all her life. She had bitterly resented things her mother did for her own good when she was a child, and her own attempts to please her mother had only made her angry. Kōko's role was still the same: the perverse, stubborn one. Yet even now she wasn't sure how this came about. For her part, all she wanted was an ordinary homely scene. She believed—or thought she believed —that lasting happiness could only be found in such surroundings, but when she told them so they would look at her in bitter perplexity. Had she been cast in this role because she'd once worshipped her brother? Was it because she had learned the meaning of life and death from a mentally retarded child? Suddenly gripped by tension, Kōko sat up very straight and placed her hand on her belly, where she could feel the stirrings again.

"Well, then," said her sister, "why don't you have your say here, first, and I'll have mine in the sitting room afterward? You can't object to that. You know, I'm not just trying to meddle. . . . "

Only half paying attention, Kōko agreed.

"As long as you . . . oh, it doesn't matter," her sister continued, "I'll tell you afterward. So, what do you want to discuss?"

Startled by the firmness of her tone, Kōko finally turned to face her and realized what she was saying. Her sister's eyes were red. Once before, Shōko had burst into tears at something Kōko had said. Kōko had been dumbfounded: she couldn't believe that she was the reason for it. As Kōko and their mother watched in silence, her sister had finally sobbed –Do you enjoy saying things like that?– Her mother had joined in: –That's right, Shōko would miss you terribly if you left us, and here you are hinting she wants you out of the way. Aren't you getting a little too big for your boots?–

Kōko had said she wanted to move into an apartment on her own. Her sister and brother-in-law had their baby, Takashi, by then, and there was much coming and going about the house. Their mother had brightened up, too. Kōko was still using the smaller room upstairs, while the married couple had the larger one, and the baby slept in their mother's room. It was an unnatural and cramped arrangement. Staying up late at night, Kōko couldn't help appearing to have the couple in the next room under surveillance, and in fact she could hear clearly if her brother-in-law so much as coughed. Kōko was sure he must feel ill at ease in the crowded household into which he'd married, and she wasn't happy herself, caught inadvertently in a tight spot.

The way she saw it, it was simple: she would be leaving home sooner or later, and if she was going to have to move into another room of the house anyway, for the couple's sake, then why not move out altogether and rent an apartment of her own? Since she'd already begun taking piano pupils, she should be able to afford the rent herself. If she was really going to set up house alone, all she had to do was take on more pupils. It was irresistible in its simplicity. In another six months she'd have finished college. Though she hadn't decided what to do after graduating, she knew she'd be working, and she'd have no money worries then. That night Kōko had told her mother and sister of her decision, adding that she wanted to move out as soon as possible, now that her mind was made up, since that would no doubt suit her sister's family too.

Kōko had completely misjudged the effect on them both: her sister had cried, and her mother had lectured her without giving her a chance to finish. Taken completely by surprise, Kōko had gazed at them, forgetting to explain what she'd meant. Both these people had been at her side ever since she was born, yet, when it came to the point, she simply didn't know what they saw or thought. And she, in turn, probably couldn't expect them to understand her. She sensed vaguely that it was weakness that made them cling even to someone like her. And though she didn't consciously identify this weakness of theirs, she saw no sense in frightening them any more than she could help.

A week later, with nothing by way of apology, she rented an apartment. Her friends lost no time in coming to see her. Both Doi and Hatanaka came to the apartment. And a year later she began to live with Hatanaka.

To some extent she had to admit, on looking back, that she mightn't have been able to leave her family quite so coolly if she hadn't been the youngest and still untested by life. It was no misfortune to Kōko that her father had loved another woman, nor that her brother was born handicapped, but perhaps her mother and sister were always lonely, always bereft, for they remembered her father and brother more clearly as part of their day-to-day lives. And that would help explain, at least a little, her sister's continuing watchfulness over her. As she said: "You're the only sister I've got, so of course I'm concerned about you." Whenever they came face to face, Kōko would be on her guard; but before she could say anything her nervousness would give way to a strangely subdued mood, for she realized the affection they shared.

Returning Shōko's gaze now, she tried to urge herself on: you can't go home today without having said anything, you absolutely must tell them about the baby. Yes, she would, but . . . she shifted her eyes to the clock on the wall.

She *would* tell, but only after hearing her sister out. She could just mention it briefly on her way out of the house. There was no need for explanations or apologies. There was still plenty of time.

Since Kōko clearly was not going to break the silence, her sister said firmly: "What's wrong? Is it so difficult to talk about? Don't worry, hardly anything would surprise me now where you're concerned."

"I'm very sorry," Kōko answered in a small voice, "but I'd like to listen to you first. What's it about?"

It was her sister's turn to fall silent. The tip of her nose was reddening, like her eyes. Kōko was reminded that she shared their mother's chronic sinus trouble. Kōko's trouble was with her ears, and her brother had been the same. But anyone could have told at a glance that they were sisters—in fact they were very alike in many ways, from their features to their manner of speaking. Kōko wanted to say so, but the confusion on her sister's face put a stop even to this stray remark.

" . . . All right, then. I expect you've just about guessed what I have to say, anyway. . . . But you don't need to beat about the bush with me, you know, not after all that we've. . . . Oh, Kōko. . . . "

Shōko's eyes suddenly widened. Kōko went rigid with embarrassment. Her sister was staring at her body again, fearfully now. Kōko gave a nod, realizing at the same moment that she wouldn't get to hear Shōko out today. Her hands, resting on the table, had started to tremble. She could only smile, no words would come. She was aware that Kayako was staring fixedly at her too, from a distance, but she couldn't make her head turn that way.

It was some time before Shōko attempted to speak. She didn't seem to know what to say, or how. Kōko waited to hear her voice, listening meanwhile to the sounds from the TV: an emcee's patter, and buzzers; a quiz show, it seemed. Shōko got up slowly.

" . . . Look, why don't you come into the other room?"

Kōko also stood and shifted her chair. "First let's talk about Kayako." She was trying to compose her expression to match her sister's seriousness, but it only crumpled further into a meaningless smile.

"How can you go on saying that?" Her sister was almost whispering, and averting her eyes.

"Doesn't Kayako's school start tomorrow?"

"That's right. And you've gone and. . . . "

"But I keep telling you, I want to attend the ceremony tomorrow, and. . . . "

"What *are* you saying? It's out of the question. Does this sort of thing amuse you?"

"Amuse me! It's just that I can't ask you to go on looking after Kayako forever, so. . . . "

"I don't know what you're getting at. What are you grinning for? Stop it, it's disgusting."

Before she knew it her sister was almost shouting. Kayako and her cousins were staring. And Kōko felt as if Kayako had thrust her away. Kayako—she wanted to say—it's not like you to be shocked so easily after all you've seen. Before she turned two, the girl had seen her parents tangling, beside themselves with emotion, and hitting and kicking each other; and she had seen her mother and Doi arguing with clenched fists, and sharing the same bed, too. Kayako had grown up that way, she was that kind of child. She wasn't some delicate hothouse plant like the children of this household. Kōko was slowly growing impatient with her sister, who stood there needing to be won over first before she'd allow her to deal directly with Kayako. Shōko wasn't about to back down—but what real help did she think she could give Kōko? And why did she constantly come between Kayako and herself? The person she wanted to talk to was Kayako.

At her sister's outburst, Kōko's silly grin finally faded.

"I intend to apologize where apologies are due. . . . But apologizing won't put things back as they were. I've always done the best I could, even if you mightn't think so. And that's all I can do in future. Though it may turn out even worse than in the past. Kayako understands. And so . . . I want you to give her back. . . . "

Faltering, she stopped and looked around. Although she hadn't seen her move, Kayako was standing beside her aunt now, watching her mother in bewilderment. She was the image of Shōko—or was it merely their expressions that were the same? That isn't *my* Kayako, she thought. Her head swam with helplessness and embarrassment. With a rush of emotion close to rage she shouted at Kayako: "What are you gawking at? How long are you going to go on sponging off your aunt? Whose child are you, for God's sake? Go and pack your bags. You're coming home with me."

Kayako covered her face in a childish gesture and burst into tears. Shōko let out a shrill cry. "Now just a minute! What nonsense is this? Calm down, will you? And sit down. You're not well, and all this excitement isn't good for you. . . . It's all right, Kaya, go to your room. Leave your mother to me, there's no need to worry."

Kōko jumped up from the dining chair where she'd been made to sit and followed doggedly after Kayako, who was doing as she was told.

"No, Kayako, listen to me!"

"Will you stop it! You've tormented her enough already! Now run along, Kaya dear."

"Don't you dare. . . . "

Gripping Kayako by the arm, Kōko dragged her back to the table. Kayako stopped crying and glared red-eyed at her mother. Kōko stared back at her. A long, firm-featured face. A mature face for her age. She was tall as well; she might have passed for fourteen. She had been a round-faced baby, with chubby cheeks that all but hid her nose and mouth. Kōko didn't know what to tell her. She gave her an uncertain smile and glanced aside at Shōko.

" . . . I'm sorry about all this."

Shōko nodded hastily in return. She was pale. "It's all right. Listen, stay here tonight. That's the best idea. Tomorrow you can go with Kayako to the school opening. Don't worry, I'll lend you a kimono. Do stay, please. Kaya would be glad, too. We're always saying so—if you'd only come back here. Mother used to say so, often. It has to be too much for you, trying to do everything by yourself. You must be tired out. Don't think I don't understand how you feel, wanting to cope on your own, but it's no good waiting till something disastrous happens and then changing your mind, is it? There's still time. . . . You can come here for a while, have a nice rest, and think things over. You've had enough troubles already. This is *your* home, too, you know, you can just march in as if you owned the place. Really, I wish you would. It would make Kaya so happy. Wouldn't it, Kaya?"

Kayako merely blinked her reddened eyes without answering. Smiling vaguely, her aunt went on: " . . . Yes, people go a little strange with no one to talk to. Too much loneliness can make you do all sorts of things. It's like an illness. So . . . no one will think the worse of you. The main thing is to get over this. . . ."

"I'm not ill," Kōko put in quickly, watching Kayako's face. Kayako had parted her lips as if to say something. Kōko could hardly wait for those lips to start moving. Don't be shy, she thought, if there's something you want to say—anything at all—go ahead and say it. She suspected she knew what it was.

" . . . Of course you're not really ill, but it's *like* an illness. If you come here and take it easy, you'll soon get better. You could keep up your piano if you wanted to, and just leave your apartment, you'll find a use for it later, for giving lessons or something. But start by having a rest here for a week, anyway, or a month, and don't worry about a thing. And then we'll be able to talk properly, too. . . ."

Her sister turned in mid-sentence toward the table, and at that moment they heard Kayako's voice, with a hoarse, pained ring to it. "I—don't want her to come. I—I hate people like her. I can't stand the sight of her."

And she ran from the room, footsteps clattering. Shōko took two or three steps in pursuit, then shrilled at her own children who hadn't budged from the TV: "What are you lot doing? Quick, go and see if Kaya's all right."

Miho leaped up and switched off the set, and Takashi hauled himself out of his chair.

"Not you, Takashi, you get on with your homework. In your second year and all you ever do is watch TV! Oh, Miho, wait, you needn't go either. Go to your room. I'm sure you can find something to do. We'd better leave Kaya on her own for a while."

The children withdrew to their bedrooms without so much as a look in Kōko's direction. Kōko surveyed the now quiet room with a curious satisfaction: so that's how they protect their world and keep it undisturbed, peaceful, and clean. Her heart went out to Kayako, who had cared enough to fling such vehemence at her.

When her sister turned back again Kōko finally saw her chance. "I ought to be going, today," she said. "I'd like to go to the school opening, for Kayako's sake, but I don't know yet. She doesn't particularly want me to, and. . . . "

"As if that mattered at a time like this! Why couldn't you have had an abortion before now? How could you leave it till you got like that! It's a nightmare." And Shōko actually began to rub her eyes hard with the fingers of one hand, as if awakening from sleep.

There was a red thread, quite a long piece, against the gray of the rug. Kōko stared at it as she spoke. "It's due in September. Kayako was born in August, so my children are all summer babies, aren't they?"

"What?"

Kōko raised her head and almost collided with a look of frank amazement. Her sister had rubbed her eyes until they watered.

" . . . The most important part of a child's experience is being involved in the mother's life. She can't be allowed just to run off when it suits her."

"Kōko, stop, stop talking this nonsense."

Her sister tottered over and sank onto the sofa. Kōko followed, to pick up her shoulder bag and cardigan. She would very much have liked to sit down, but she suspected she'd never make it home if she did. She knew the old sofa well: its dark blue depths were almost treacherously soft. Hatanaka used to sit there, once. And Kōko had taken midsummer naps there in her student days, lying drenched with sweat.

" . . . Well, then, I'll be on my way. . . . We still have to talk about Kayako, so I'll come again another time."

Kōko hurried to the hallway before her sister could muster a reply.

95

When she saw her down-at-heel shoes lined up neatly just inside the door, she let out a deep breath that was almost a sigh. Before her sister could appear from the living room she put them on, opened the door, and went out.

In the chill air she felt as though she were standing on a quiet beach. The shrubbery, which formed dark blue silhouettes, made watery rustling sounds. The gravel at her feet seemed to give off a bluish-white phosphorescence. No cars passed along the residential street. A faint sound rumbled in the distance, like faraway thunder.

Kōko took a single breath, filling her lungs, and started to run, determined to make it to the main road. But her lumpish body wasn't up to it. She tried to keep running all the same from plain stubbornness. At the back of her mind she could see the figure of a child scampering along a broad seashore. It was her, aged ten, looking just like Kayako. Far ahead was the running figure of her brother. Kōko watched, light at heart, as the quiet shore spread out in a monotone before her. The scene opened out rapidly to the sides, like Cinemascope; the little point in the very middle was herself. A crisp, chilly breeze. Her brother, far away. The sound of waves, and their footsteps. Two sets of footsteps. No, there was another: someone was behind her. She looked back as she ran. Kayako—six years old—was running, yelling something. She was black from head to foot—coated, probably, with sand that had stuck to her wet skin. Wait, Mommy, *wait*: Kayako's voice came through the lulls between waves. Kōko faced ahead again and put on speed. Her brother was looking back and waving. But it wasn't him. It seemed to be Doi. Doi was waving. No, it was a boy she'd never seen before. Or perhaps she had met him somewhere, but she couldn't think where. And they were careering along, the boy and her, so fast that everything became a blur. They might have been in tiny vacuum tubes skimming horizontally along the shore. The three of them gradually drew further apart. . . . Kayako's voice trailed away. . . . And Kayako had faded into the sand. But Kayako is me, she thought. Yes, I am Kayako . . . yet I've abandoned her.

Kōko picked up a taxi on the main street.

As it moved off there was a sharp pain in her abdomen and a film of gold dust bleared her eyes. She stopped the taxi and got out. Unable to see anything for the haze, she groped to the guardrail and crouched, gripping it with both hands. She wondered briefly what had caused the pain—well, what do you expect, she thought, dashing around like that—yet her body mattered less than the seaside scene. She could have sworn she'd actually been there. Was it with her mother and brother? But they'd never gone on holiday as a family, so how could she have run with him beside the sea? Had she forgotten some day at the beach with Doi and Kayako? Or was she mixing it up with an outing that Hatanaka had taken them on?

Hatanaka came from a small town by the Japan Sea, and they had gone on a trip there when Kayako was still a baby. But there had been no sandy beach. It was an utterly bleak fishing port, squarely concreted over. They had left the seafront after five minutes because the wind was too strong for the baby, though Hatanaka had specially wanted to take them there. The sea was dark, without motion, giving no sense of space.

She waited patiently for the cramps to subside, searching her memory in the meantime for some other beach—and before she knew it she had dozed off.

When she came to, both the pain and the gold dust were gone.

Kōko set off on foot through a part of town she had never visited. The stores were still open: when she peered into one and checked a clock, she found that it wasn't fifteen minutes since she left her sister's house.

5

While the opening ceremony was in progress at Kayako's school, Kōko was asleep in her apartment. Sounds echoed about her ears: the pounding of mattresses hung out to air, car horns in the street below, patriotic music blaring from a sound truck. She felt she was sleeping inside a tiny box perched atop a streetlight. Its clear glass sides reflected the morning light in such a golden sheen that the bed where Kōko lay was invisible to people passing in the street.

In a half-waking dream, she pursued the image of herself—busy day and night—once the baby was born. This time next year he'd be seven months old and beginning to crawl. He'd be teething, too. That's when they always squirm and fret having their diapers changed, she thought. I'll grab his legs as he tries to crawl away, smack his little buttocks with their bluish birthmark, and tell him firmly: no, come on, hold still.

Kayako—I'll call—bring a clean diaper.

Here. . . . Goodness, what a row! Crybaby! Ooh, what a horrid face!

But he looks just like you when he does that, Kayako. There, doesn't that feel better? . . . Look, he's laughing now.

Now, take Baby off to bed and I'll bring his bottle right away.

I'm not sleepy yet. I want to play some more.

Oh, no, you don't. If you stay up late the bogeyman will get you.

No, he won't. When I'm in bed you'll both have nice things to eat. I've seen you.

What have you seen?

The baby gives a resounding yell.

What's the matter with him?

Nothing—he probably hasn't had enough milk.

Kōko takes up the baby in her arms, and finds herself in a park at night. Doi, looking strangely old, comes up and speaks to her.

My, hasn't he grown! He looks exactly like Kayako.

Kayako has climbed to the top of the jungle gym, where she's singing Brahms's Lullaby.

Of course. They're both my children, after all.

Half yours. There is a strong likeness, for two kids who are only half yours, but I didn't really mean "exactly," I was just being polite. Don't let it go to your head.

They're both mine and mine only.

Come off it!

I'm not causing anyone else any trouble.

You're causing the children a pack of trouble just by keeping them alive.

No, I'm not. . . . How can you talk like that when you're alive yourself? The children are grateful to me, really.

You're very sure of yourself.

I have to be.

Are you having a good time, cuddling him and all that?

You're full of snide remarks these days, aren't you?

I'm not as young as I was. But how is it working out? Has it been a compensation, like you thought?

Just look at him and you can see for yourself.

He's scrawny.

Yes, he never sleeps. His eyes are always open.

That figures.

Why do you say that?

My kid—you remember when we had him—he's just the same. Kids aren't something you want to have for special reasons. Even I finally came to realize that. And you, why did you decide to have one now?

99

I waited and waited and no one turned up, so I thought, well, in that case, the only thing to do is to have a child myself.

What are you talking about? You walked out on me. Why did you take off for so little reason?

But, there was your child. . . .

What of it? Do you really think kids count for all that much?

But they're so lovable.

Well, even I can see that, with my kid being so strange. But where does that leave you? No matter how many kids you have, parents are still on their own. Everyone knows that. All you're doing, in the end, is clinging to them as something easier to handle, and trying to forget how ugly it can get—isn't that so? How do you manage without a man? Did having a baby like this do you any good at all? Well?

No. None. But he's so sweet. Look, he's smiling at you.

He's repulsive.

What a thing to say!

But it's true, and I can tell you because I think of him as my child, too.

He's not your child.

Come on, hand him over, it's about time. His mother's waiting at home.

No! I won't let him go!

In a panic Kōko tries to escape with the baby. At the same time Kayako comes running toward her from the jungle gym, a streak of silver—an old-fashioned scimitar—held aloft in her right hand and her face flaming with anger.

Kayako would destroy the baby, too, if she had a chance. Why is everyone after him?

Because he's a fake. Doi's booming voice follows Kōko as she turns and runs.

Have mercy! she cries. He's such a dear little thing. Let him alone! Over her own voice she hears Kayako's, but deeper now—an adult's voice very like Hatanaka's.

As she flees, Kōko thinks: the baby hasn't a chance like this. I should ditch it. But now I've gone and had it, it's too late to cancel that. Too late. . . .

She was suddenly afraid of the infant in her arms. She wanted to let go. It was so dreadful she couldn't bear to look. But her hands had melted into the baby's flesh as if squeezing an overripe banana.

All the strength left Kōko's body in one rush of despair. She heaved herself up, gasping for breath, as though crawling from a swamp. Seeing the familiar layout of her own room she breathed more easily: she was safe. Then she rubbed the curve of her belly with both hands.

She got out of bed, went into the kitchen in her nightgown, and opened the window. The sky was high and clear. She was about to turn on the faucet when she discovered a small brown bug lying on its back where it must have fallen from the stack of dishes, waving its legs in a desperate effort to right itself. The dishes had been sitting in the sink for two days. Curry was caked hard on the dinner plate. Kōko turned the tap full on with her eyes on the insect. The water cascaded over it and flushed it, still wriggling, down the drain. Kōko stayed watching the stream of water.

That afternoon she reached the music store half an hour early. It was lunchtime, and the office was empty. She unlocked the practice room labeled "A" and went in. After surveying the inside of the store through the window she sat down at the piano. She opened the lid, took a sheet of music from the rack at her elbow, and set it up on the piano. It was a Handel minuet. She began to play: the simple melody suggested a child skipping barefoot over gentle spring meadows. Her touch was light enough, but she kept making mistakes. Why did just one wrong note make the whole effect so disturbing? Kōko took her hands from the keyboard and laid them in her lap, but continued to follow the written music with her eyes. The minuet played on peacefully in her head.

The family's old piano had stood in the sitting room near a bay window that opened onto a vine-covered trellis, and she and her brother used to hang out of the window to pick handfuls of small grapes and pop them in their mouths. The grapes were all caught up in spiders' webs that gave a dusty, gritty feel to the inside of her mouth—she took it for their flavor. Her brother gobbled them down, skin, seeds, and all. There was a dog kennel under the trellis, and the dog was always barking at the children.

A while later the door opened to admit her first pupil of the day.

After stopping for a meal on the way home, she arrived at her door to find it unlocked. She went in, wondering if she'd forgotten again to lock up, and there was her sister installed in the kitchen.

"I was just about to leave, you took so long to get here," she said. "Do you always get home about now?"

Kōko nodded and dropped her shoulder bag onto the table. The TV was on.

"Did you get the key from Kayako?"

"Yes. Don't be upset. I knew you wouldn't agree to see me, anyway, if I asked you."

"Oh? . . . Why should you think that?" With a stiff smile Kōko walked around the table to the refrigerator.

"You were looking daggers at me yesterday. . . . I went to Kaya's opening. You know, she did seem lonely, after all. . . . "

"Oh, thanks. . . . Do you realize, this is the first time you've ever been to see me here." Kōko took a bottle of beer from the refrigerator.

"It's rather nice, isn't it?"

"Yes, I've got you to thank for that. Will you have a beer?"

"Oh—no, it's all right. I can't stay long."

"Just one won't hurt." She put a glass in front of her and filled it. After pouring another for herself she poked about in the refrigerator till she found an unopened package of blue cheese, which she put on the table.

"I'm afraid that's all there is. . . . But you and I have always liked strong-smelling things, haven't we?—dried squid, and even that stinking

102

dried mackerel, *kusaya*. I was amazed, when I grew up, to learn that most people detest the stuff."

"It was Mother's example. Funny she should've had a taste for that sort of thing, when she wasn't a drinker. I hardly ever have it myself, these days.... But, listen.... " Shōko lowered her voice.

Kōko spoke quickly: "I wonder if everyone thinks childhood was the best time of their lives? Even though I desperately wanted to escape, I knew so little of the outside world that I took Mother's word for it when she called *kusaya* a special treat. Those were happy times, you know—the thought of those 'treats' is enough to make me nostalgic. It makes me realize that for all my thinking and acting big I was really a child all along. An ordinary, childish child.... Don't you think there's something endearing about a kid with one parent liking exactly the same sort of food?"

"I think it's horrible.... " Shōko spoke in a murmur, staring at her glass. Kōko fixed her eyes on her sister and continued.

"I wonder what it would've been like if Father had been there? Mother always looked as though she'd taken on all the worries of the world, but, you know, I think she may have been happy with things as they were, because it gave her a free hand in raising her children.... I've often thought so, bringing up Kayako. Sometimes I find myself talking to Kayako exactly as Mother did to us, and it's a shock to realize that I'm my mother's daughter. I suppose if Father had been alive I wouldn't have taken after Mother quite so much. We're stubborn, we solo mothers, we like to have our own way.... What about you?"

"Look, what it boils down to is this: it isn't right for just one parent to raise a child. The least you can do is come to us."

Kōko broke in quickly, her eyes flicking to the TV screen. "But I don't want to forget that I grew up the same way. If it wasn't right then, I don't want to be right now.... "

Her sister fell silent. Kōko went on watching television, letting the silence lengthen. She hadn't seen this soap opera before, but the actors were familiar. After a pause her sister opened her handbag and placed a sheet of notepaper on the table which Kōko, her face still turned to the TV, pretended not to notice.

"We're not really getting anywhere, arguing like this, so I think I'll go home. You're an adult, in years if nothing else, and I hope you'll give it some careful thought. Look, here's a doctor I know. He's well qualified, you needn't worry about anything going wrong, and he keeps things confidential, so go and see him tomorrow if you feel like it. You're too far along to take chances with just any old doctor. . . . I've already mentioned you, so all you have to do is go, and not take it too seriously. I was told you should stay at least three days in the hospital if you can, but, well, you can discuss that when you get there. . . . You're thirty-six, and you can hardly expect your big sister, at forty-three, to drag you along to a doctor. . . . You will go, though, won't you? . . . Kaya doesn't know about you yet, so you needn't worry. You are Kaya's guardian, whether you like it or not, so something's wrong when you act as if you need a guardian yourself, at your age. No one can take responsibility for your actions. Fancy not even going to see your child start her new school! You know, if you want someone to take care of you, you should find yourself another husband . . . but take your time. It's worth thinking about, anyway. . . . Well, I must be off. . . . "

Kōko rose to see her sister out.

When Shōko turned in the doorway after putting her shoes on, Kōko asked something that had just occurred to her. "Have you been to that doctor, too?"

Shōko went pale and her mouth opened. Taken aback, for she hadn't meant to imply anything, Kōko flashed a hesitant smile. The door swung open and shut, her sister was gone. But Kōko felt the light of her eyes, the glare of hatred they had given her, still there at the door. She remembered Mrs. Doi's eyes. When was it? Was it that time she'd visited them, among a group of Doi's friends, before the first child was born? Or perhaps they weren't eyes she'd ever really seen. Though she seldom dreamed about Doi, for a time she'd encountered his wife in one dream after another; she made no accusations, but merely stared, unaware that the woman meeting her gaze was Kōko, and letting her loathing show all the more clearly because of it.

Kōko sat down in front of the TV again and had another beer. The soap opera ended and the weather forecast began. Tomorrow was likely to be another fine day.

"No one's pleased...." Kōko tried murmuring the words aloud. "No one's pleased."

She murmured them again, and added in her heart: but I don't care. A chill ran through her. She would have liked some *kusaya*, now that her sister had jogged her memory. The thought of it made her want to break down and cry. It was mean of her sister: why couldn't she have joined in and chatted about old times? She braced herself and got to her feet. She wouldn't cry now, that could wait a little longer. She stood there thinking a moment and then picked up the telephone. She already had a finger in the dial when she found she couldn't remember the number, and had to rummage through her bag for her address book. She dialed carefully, not taking her eyes from the page. Her body seemed to float like an air bladder. Or, rather, the whole room seemed to be floating on air. The unnaturally luminous tanks of the aquarium came to mind. No doubt they would still be there in the same rows if I went back; it was only six years ago. Kayako was six, and I was thirty. The fishes' names. Pirarucu. Nile lungfish. Spotted gar. Alligator gar.

The ringing signal continued. In the two-room apartment she was calling, four rings should have been ample time to pick up the receiver. As she heard the signal burring five, six times, she knew there was nobody home, and she slowly grew bolder. She held on tight and let the phone ring on and on. She had the feeling that letting it shrill for longer than necessary in the empty apartment was somehow a violation of that person's property, even though it would pass undetected. It was her first such crime in a long while. She used to call Doi's house when she knew no one was there and let the phone ring perhaps twenty times before replacing the receiver, satisfied.

Doi didn't keep secrets from her unnecessarily; after all, they'd been friends from student days. And Kōko didn't mind being told. It meant she knew quite a number of things: when his wife would be away with her parents, how his child had hurt himself, who had visited them at home. In fact she'd felt she knew all about them, and thought this gave her an advantage, which was why the news that Doi's wife was pregnant had shaken her so badly.

The pirarucus. Fish like dinosaurs, six feet long, that she and Kayako and Doi had seen together. Their black scales glowed a vivid pink where they caught the light. The small pool holding them was in a dark corner of the aquarium. They seemed close enough to reach out and touch, too big to be kept swimming in a tank like that. Or not so much swimming as nosing through the water like torpedoes. Had there been five of them, or six? Kayako had been afraid to go closer than a yard or so. And Doi had swept her up and thrust her out over the railing so she could view the pirarucus from above. Kayako had struggled and screamed fit to bust every pane of glass in the place.

–The pirarucus would have liked you to say hello– a disappointed Doi had said, setting Kayako down on the floor.

The aquarium building was dark inside. Perhaps that was why the pirarucus seemed on the verge of slithering out of the tiny pool and swarming around them; the idea was even more sinister than their appearance.

She remembered telling Kayako a while ago that she was afraid of water. She imagined blue water flooding into the room, bringing the pirarucus with it, and the black and pink torpedoes circling her. It seemed so imminent that she had to shut her eyes. She'd be all right, she thought, if it would all freeze solid.

Just then the sound of the phone she'd left ringing broke off and a man's voice burst upon her ear.

"Hello? . . . Hello? . . . "

In spite of the shock—she hadn't bargained on this happening—Kōko managed to speak up at once and sound tolerably calm.

"Hello . . . Mr. Osada? Mizuno here. I'm sorry to call you at this hour."

"Is that you, Kōko? It's not so late. I just got home this minute. I was lucky to make it in time."

"Oh, yes? . . . er. . . . How are you?"

Osada chuckled into the phone. "As you can hear, I'm fine, terrific in fact. And you, Kōko?"

"Me too . . . or maybe not, I'm not sure."

Osada laughed again. His laughter was catching, but Kōko hastened to set straight what she'd said. "I'm fine, of course, though I wouldn't say terrific."

Kōko felt vastly relieved, felt saved in fact: Osada was a friend of hers, after all, and not a bad one at that. With his nervousness and his weak health went an openness that Kōko always found reassuring. It was the feeling that a small boy gave.

"I see. Not the best, but not too bad either, eh? And how's Kaya?"

"Fine. She's already in junior high school. She's grown so fast."

"Hm. Compared to her, I guess we adults haven't changed a bit."

"I guess not. . . . Well, um. . . . " Kōko fumbled for words. She couldn't quite remember why she'd had that sudden urge to phone him or what she'd meant to say.

"What's up? Something to pass on to Hatanaka?"

"No, it's not that. . . . "

"What is it? It's not like you to be tongue-tied. . . . I ran into Hatanaka the other day."

"Really? How was he?" Kōko asked, her voice brightening for an instant.

"Fine. Yes, doing very well. He's been made head of the sales section. And put on a little more weight."

"They make gardening tools, don't they?"

"That's right. He's got his heart in his work, you know—which is all to the good."

"Mm."

"People do change, don't they? It must be nearly ten years now, isn't it?"

"Eight. Not so long, really." She was surprised in fact to note what a small number it was.

"Eight years, is it? . . . So, did you have something you wanted to talk to me about? If you'd rather we met, that's okay with me."

"Mm, that would be. . . . No, I can't meet you. And. . . . "

"You're not making yourself very clear."

"Making what clear?" she asked, blushing against the receiver.

"You don't sound your usual self today, Kōko. What's wrong with meeting?"

"It's . . . you'd know if we met."

"But I won't know if we can't meet."

"That's true. . . . " Kōko laughed hastily.

"I'll come over right away, if you like."

Osada's voice was heavy, now, as though submerged. The pirarucus started to swim again at Kōko's feet.

"Oh, no . . . I don't want to see you. It's not about Hatanaka, you know. But it's nothing to do with you, either. Honestly, nothing at all. . . . So it's all right. I'm sorry. I can't talk now. I'll phone you again."

"Just a minute. . . . Isn't Kaya there? Has something happened? . . . "

Osada's voice broke off. As she heard him catch his breath, Kōko suddenly regained her composure. Glancing around the room—there wasn't a drop of water—she told Osada: "Yes, it's Kayako, she comes out with all sorts of awkward notions. Girls are so difficult. . . . But please don't worry, I just wanted someone to listen to my woes. I don't know how I could have phoned you about something so trivial. It was silly of me. . . . Er, let's have a talk next time we see each other. . . . Bye. . . . "

Kōko hung up before Osada could get in another word. She'd been made aware, for the first time, that this was something she couldn't tell him. It stood to reason, if she was going to keep the baby on her own.

Kōko went into Kayako's room and sat down at the desk. Switching on the lamp, she gazed at a postcard of a white flower that was pinned up on the wall. It was a photograph of an alpine plant: just one flower, its pale petals spread against an out-of-focus green. Kayako had bought it herself on last year's school trip. She'd bought Kōko a souvenir too—a lucky-charm doll with tiny bells that jingled.

Kōko had gone to see Kayako off at the station where her class was assembling for the trip. The pupils waiting in the square outside had segregated neatly into two islands, girls with girls, boys with boys, and the two groups were humming with excitement in the tones of their own sex, which seemed to add enormously to the fun. Taken one by one, however, the children could be seen watching the other island with sharp little animal eyes. In view of their age, though—eleven or twelve—this was a normal, healthy scene. Kayako's first menstruation had come three months earlier. Many of the boys' voices were breaking. They were at that age. All that the adults need do was stand back and watch these children, fondly, and a little nostalgically.

But Kōko had to look away. What did it mean, this compulsive awareness of the other sex as children grew up? Let their breasts fill out and their voices break, well and good; but why must they be so acutely sensitive to the other sex that they hadn't time to heed the changes in themselves? While Kayako was clinging bodily to the girls' island, her mind was clearly on the boys: she appeared especially nervous of them, and especially self-conscious, regardless of whether anyone was actually looking her way. Kōko couldn't help being irritated. And a glance around her—at the beaming smiles of the other women, who were wives as well as mothers—was still more provoking, because it suggested a possible reason for her jaundiced view of the children. Was she eyeing them so ungenerously because she had no link of her own with the opposite sex?

Hers was an unreasoning anger: she wasn't pleased to discover that she was not the only one who dwelled so fixedly on the existence of men. She was unable to deny the evidence of her own nature, though, for she knew (at the risk of being called obsessed with sex) that this greedy desire of hers had indeed been there since childhood, differing little from an adult's. Sex had never been far away even when she was playing with her brother; in fact it was the source of the delight she took in him. And when she was younger still, she had dreamed of being cuddled and babied by the father she didn't remember. The pleasure she felt then, too, was sexual.

As she buried her face in Doi's bare chest she would turn suddenly defiant: if I was born this way, what's the use in trying to change now? She supposed she had Kayako's good at heart, and yet she could never guarantee that she wouldn't abandon her in some remote place if it were the only way she could have Doi. The selfishness of it chilled her even as she clung naked to him. But it was Doi who'd made her feel alive at last, after those years of deadened intimacy with the husband she'd just lost. She hadn't spared a thought for Doi's wife, though she ought to have known well enough what it was like to have her husband taken from her. Meeting Doi again had taught her that, in this respect, she too was in the grip of instincts that had no place in the rational scheme of things: sharp claws and fangs were bared in self-protection. The knowledge brought her close to tears, and yet somehow she made herself strangely at home with it.

But had she been the rule, and not the exception, in all this? She was convinced she saw sexuality in the children's overloud laughter, the way they hugged and slapped one another's shoulders, the way they doubled up with giggles. It all began with just such an awareness of the other sex's presence: they would begin to hold hands, and very soon their bodies would be locked together, then they'd have children of their own and their confidence in their own sex would grow till they became like the matrons who'd escorted them there. "Human being" was a fine-sounding phrase; but did it ever mean more than lust incarnate? Was that all there was to it? Kōko had felt as though something she'd trusted in, a kind of salvation, had been taken from her.

No, she could see now that her mind must have been twisted if sexuality was all she could find, even for a moment, in that happy gathering

110

of children. For only a day later she had met Osada and enjoyed that sensual warmth. And now she was carrying a five-month fetus. She wondered how she would have reacted to the same scene now, feeling sure the pregnancy had changed her point of view.

Kōko stayed sitting in Kayako's chair.

After half an hour she finally got up and took a shower, washing with elaborate care. She lathered her round belly in circular, stroking motions with the palm of her hand.

After putting on her nightgown Kōko poured herself a whiskey. Every time she heard footsteps ringing in the corridor outside, she stared tensely at the door. Every time, the steps went right past. She knew Osada wouldn't come to see her simply because she'd phoned like that, and yet she couldn't quite give up hope. I mustn't behave as though I'm expecting him, Kōko told herself. There's no point in making myself miserable. But how do I know that actively waiting mightn't work on his body like a magnet, drawing him here? And so she put off crawling into bed. She was exasperated with herself for first phoning and then, typically, being unable to come to the point. It had been their first phone call in four months.

Kōko checked over what she'd said. Perhaps it had sounded no different from her other calls, where the names of Hatanaka and Kayako always came out seeming like mere pretexts for the claims of sexual desire. Certainly her calls had sounded like that in the past. Osada was always clear-cut on that point: for him meeting Kōko meant having sex. And Kōko hadn't sought anything extra from him, for wasn't it enough that each time they met he gave her all the solace he could, however mistaken about her he might be?

Osada didn't try to hide from her the shyness and inferiority he still felt in a woman's presence, like a pubescent boy. He couldn't see her purely in terms of the opposite sex, for Kōko had been Hatanaka's wife. He seemed to count on her indulgence when he told her about the twenty-nine-year-old he hoped to marry, or the nurse, just turned twenty, with whom he said he was in love; it seemed he was so timid toward

111

them both that they regarded him as just a softhearted friend. Kōko only half listened to these stories, controlling the hurt that welled inside
her. And since Osada expected it of her, she would throw her arms
around his plump body in a show of feeling that she knew was over-
done, but believed necessary all the same.

Just this once, though—her temper rising as the alcohol took effect—she couldn't stand to be misinterpreted in the usual way. She was
having a baby. She wanted to drum into his belly, through the layer of
fat, that desire never ends in desire alone. She couldn't help thinking
that she might already be remote from sex. Perhaps pregnancy was like
that. Though of course she'd been afraid of getting pregnant, perhaps
somewhere in her heart she had wanted it as a means of survival.
Strangely, her self-respect hadn't allowed her to avoid conception
throughout another affair. She didn't want to go on living inside the
limits of sexual relations with men.

It might have been her age, thirty-six, that made Kōko think like this.
She was proud of her resolve. The only way she could escape the molten
lava of her own sexuality had been to conceive and have the baby. And
when she remembered the looks she'd had from Osada and her sister,
and Doi and Hatanaka before them, it was with anger this time. Giving
birth to this baby was the only way to show Doi why she wouldn't
become pregnant during her time with him, and how badly she had
wanted to escape the power of sex. To Doi her body must have seemed
as safe as mud.

Letting her drunkenness lead her on, Kōko called Osada again. The
phone rang on unanswered.

His absence didn't imply he was on his way. Instead, she sensed indifference. They only remembered each other at the sound of the other's
voice; that was all there had ever been between them.

With the receiver still pressed to her ear, Kōko muttered: I must go to
a hospital tomorrow. The only one that came to mind was the university
hospital where she'd had Kayako.

6

The doorbell chimed just as Kōko was putting on her shoes. She was still feeling the effects of the night's drunkenness. Who the hell can that be at this hour of the morning?—and when I'm in a hurry, too—she was thinking as she opened the door. It was Osada. For a moment, in her astonishment, she thought something must have happened to Hatanaka. She forgot that she'd done anything herself. But the sound of Osada's voice—as startled as a child uncapping a jack-in-the-box —brought back her phone call of the night before. "I haven't much time," she said, flustered, "but come in, anyway."

When he was seated in the kitchen, it finally seemed to register that the change in Kōko's appearance wasn't just extra weight. Kōko was so intent on following his expression that she didn't even offer him a cup of coffee. Osada looked very young for his age, perhaps because he'd stayed single, but now, as she studied his profile, his features hardened in a look more suited to his years. Kōko was glad to see it: at least he would spare her the kind of emotional outburst she might expect from someone in his twenties.

". . . The baby has already started to move. I've been thinking I ought to tell you. I'm sorry. Today's a bad day, though—I don't have time to explain properly. . . . I can bring the child up on my own, without having to bother you at all—as long as *you* don't let it worry you, I mean."

In a rush, Kōko explained as fully as she could that Osada's own status was not affected in any way under the law, that she meant to ensure he

113

wouldn't be affected, that she wanted to forget about the child's father herself and raise it on her own.

Osada remained silent. He gazed steadily at the table. He didn't hold his head in his hands and bemoan his luck, as Hatanaka might have done, nor did he look the other way and puff a cigarette, like Doi.

Kōko got up, her eyes on the clock. "I have to go soon. . . . "

Osada lifted his head and looked directly at her. Even then he said nothing. His lips were dry.

Kōko said, "Shall we leave together?"

Osada got clumsily to his feet and fixed her round belly with that glowering stare.

He finally spoke once they reached the street.

"Are you on your way to work?"

The street outside was filled with morning light. Half closing her eyes, Kōko looked up at the young leaves on the trees lining the sidewalk.

"Not until the afternoon," she answered. "I'm on my way to the hospital."

"The hospital?"

The fresh leaves would glisten as long as the early light lasted.

"Today's my first time."

"Oh. . . . Well, anyway, take care."

Kōko looked at Osada: his eyes too were crinkling in the light. She thought he was going to smile, but he went on regarding her with a hint of sourness about his mouth. Disappointed, she glanced away at a parked car.

"I'm tough. . . . Please don't worry. Honestly. Not worrying is the best thing you can possibly do for me. . . . Because then I can think of this child as really mine alone. . . . "

"A sort of virgin birth?"

"Well, sort of. . . . Though it's too late to say so now without sounding preposterous."

"It *is* preposterous."

"But I wonder if it's too much to ask that just one person should

114

believe it? Everyone is so down-to-earth, I'm sick of it, they've all got one-track minds."

For the first time Osada broke into a grin.

"What do you mean, one-track minds?"

Kōko smiled back.

'. . . Never mind. . . . Well, I catch the bus over there. . . . "

Osada saw where she was pointing and nodded. "Okay, then . . . I may give you a call. . . . I can't say just now. . . . "

"It has been rather sudden. . . . "

"A virgin birth, eh?"

They parted laughing. As soon as Kōko turned her back on Osada and walked away, though, her heart sank: that was all for today, but there was next time. . . .

She had to hurry to catch her bus. When it moved off in the direction Osada had taken on foot, Kōko searched the sidewalk hoping to catch sight of him, but to no avail.

Closing her eyes, she leaned back in the seat and drifted off till she heard her stop announced. She had no qualms now, she was simply sleepy after getting up so early. Trips to the hospital had meant an early start the last time, too, when she was expecting Kayako, and she was always overcome with drowsiness in the waiting room. She had treated herself like an invalid—though she'd only been twenty-four—and slept and slept. She was an expectant mother: that was the one thought in her mind. Not the prospect of seeing the newborn's face, for never having had a baby of her own she had no idea what it would be like. It had been strange to draw steadily nearer something unimaginable, and she had stared endlessly at her body.

Thickly muffled in weariness, she was glad she would soon slip into the same routine. From now on she would think of nothing but her womb. She would get plenty of sleep, plenty of nourishment, think of names, and prepare baby clothes. This time she wanted to give the baby all the loving she could. This time, there would be no regrets. Just as long as the baby came safely into the world, she didn't care if she, the mother, were left an empty shell. Her child would feel proud to be alive if he knew how intently his mother had awaited his arrival. She promised him that much, regardless of what kind of future she would be able to give him. He might be born terribly handicapped, but that mustn't stop him growing up proud. Let him grow up arrogant and ruthless, she thought, with Kayako and me to watch over him. Especially if he's retarded like my brother. No one is going to force him to live in servile deference to other people's wishes.

The hospital was crowded, as always, but her turn to see the doctor came around sooner than expected. Kōko, who had been staring curiously at the pregnant women in the waiting room—even though she was one of them, with her belly protruding as plainly as theirs—started when her name was called so quickly, and in jerking to her feet she dropped her shoulder bag on the floor. She scraped up its spilled contents and entered the examination room, shrinking with embarrassment.

The room had changed little since her visits before Kayako was born. It had been newly redecorated at the time, and the only change, if it could be called that, was twelve years' wear and tear. The cream-colored linoleum, once perilously slippery, was now so worn that the concrete showed underneath.

Another half-hour went by before her name was called again in a curtained-off area. Once inside the curtains Kōko removed her stockings and lay down on the examination table. First a nurse measured her abdomen with a tape and checked with both hands for the fetal position. This took a long time, however, as she seemed to have difficulty locating the fetus. A doctor arrived and began to palpate the uterus, but he too gave a puzzled look.

"How many weeks is it, again?" the young doctor asked.

The nurse answered first: "Twenty-one."

"Odd, perhaps it's undersized. We'll have an X-ray taken later, if necessary. Now, let's check the heartbeat."

He switched on a small machine beside the bed and pressed a

microphone attachment onto Kōko's abdomen. She'd listened to the heart on the same machine when she was having Kayako and knew the sound to expect: a restless fluttering, like the scuttling of a mouse. The first signal a mother receives directly from her child. Anxious that the thudding of her own pulse might interfere with the machine, she managed at least to breathe quietly as she strained toward the speaker, alert for the baby's signal.

The doctor was placing the microphone here and there on her abdomen and tilting his head in a puzzled fashion. All that emerged from the speaker was static like the roar of the sea. Kōko lifted her head and joined the doctor in peering at her belly. She was fretting with impatience while the fetus took its time as if, like a baby's smile, the heartbeat were something it could give or not, just as it pleased. This is no time to play hard-to-get, she pleaded, you'll have us both in trouble if you don't get on with it. At any moment, she feared, the doctor might wrongfully reach a conclusion that would crush them both. Just a little signal would do. Barely knowing what she was doing, she flexed and unflexed her abdominal muscles, bent her legs, tried everything that might help.

"This is no good. We'll do an internal examination," said the doctor, switching off the machine.

Kōko sat up briskly and asked: "What's the situation?"

"Well, we can't tell yet. This happens often enough. A thick layer of subcutaneous fat can make diagnosis very difficult. Now, I'd like you to wait till you're called over there."

Kōko stepped down with a helping hand from the nurse. She sat on a bench opposite the internal examination room and awaited the next stage. Now's the time if you're going to run, she thought, but it was too much effort to get to her feet. There couldn't be anything wrong. There hadn't been any bleeding. She should know. She was overweight, that was all. She would simply disappoint the doctor by failing to present any problem in the internal examination, and once the bed was booked for the delivery there'd be no need to come again for quite some time.

A pale wisp of a girl was sitting next to her: she looked about high school age. Whatever could have happened inside her, Kōko wondered with vague concern. Nobody came to this university hospital for an ordinary abortion. On the other side of the girl sat a woman obviously close to term, resting her hands uncomfortably on her belly. Kōko's heart refused to be quiet. She was having trouble breathing, and she couldn't see much, either. There'd been nothing untoward during her checkups with Kayako; everything had passed so smoothly that she'd almost wished more would happen.

There was a window across the way. Through racks of assorted instruments outlined against the panes she could see a distant wall, with its own rows of windows lit by the sun. They evidently belonged to the wards: towels and underwear fluttered over the sills, and spots of color in flowerpots caught her eye. The angle of the wall left half of the window filled by blue sky and a treetop—thin branches wavering like a sapling's. In fact, though, any tree that reached that fourth-floor window must have been massive. Kōko was tempted to go and find out just how big it was. The round leaves were shimmering whitely like flakes of metal. She didn't recall seeing it when she was last there.

She remembered again that it was spring. The thought made her long to stretch, to luxuriate, to run in the light, to feel the season as it should be felt. Like the hours spent playing in the vacant lot with her brother. Or that day, on a school outing in spring, when she'd run barefoot on a sandy beach. . . .

Kōko snapped wide awake: *that* was when she raced off along the shore. Not with Doi, nor her brother, nor Kayako. She remembered straggling behind when the class reassembled on the beach at the appointed hour, and on a sudden willful impulse running on barefoot, deliberately getting farther from the group, though the time to assemble was long since past. She didn't want to see anyone's face ever again. She knew that no amount of chatting and girlish pranks and all the perfectly ordinary things she did in junior high would satisfy the hunger she felt. She was aware that the boys in her class were somehow sorry for her, knowing the situation at home, but at the same time they were wary of her, considering it safer not to get too close. She was a plain, thin girl who often contrived to draw attention to herself. She would dash out of the classroom in the middle of a lesson, ignore her turn to sweep the floor, sing loudly but leave the dustpan and broom untouched. One way or another she took great pains, for no particular reason, to ensure that people kept their distance.

If there's no one I can really talk to, then you might as well leave me alone, was what she seemed to be saying. The fair-mindedness of everyone at school, their concern that no child should ever be left out, drove her wild.

I was like that then, thought Kōko as she gazed at the blue sky half filling the window. When I ran along the beach I was hoping a "bad man" would come and spirit me away. What could a "bad man" do, anyway? At worst, he could only fiddle with this stupid body. And then he'd take me to an unimaginable world of brimming colors, a world without pretense..

She hadn't found her "bad man," though; instead, the teacher had chased after her and put an end to her mischief. She simply pretended to have forgotten the assembly time. Which didn't help change anything. She still went to school; the schoolgirl pranks continued.

And I still haven't changed a thing, Kōko murmured to herself.

From the time she was summoned till her return to the apartment, Kōko watched herself as remotely as she might her early childhood: with a sharp pang of loss, but only a faint sense of reality.

First the doctor said, in a kind of groan, ". . . Not a thing."

Then a large man with close-cropped hair, whom the first doctor addressed as the head of the department, took a look inside and muttered, "Nothing, it's true."

After that Kōko had to sit facing the two doctors in a small office. She would have no memory, afterward, of her own responses to what was said. She was suspicious of the doctors: how could they be genuine

119

when they talked such fantastic nonsense? And she suspected that the time she was spending there was not what it seemed, either. She couldn't help thinking that something had come unstuck.

Clearly, time and space must have buckled out of their true linearity into curves that doubled back and fused together, all without her noticing. Then what was this time, this space? They were an illusion. Nothing but tangled strings. She must keep her wits about her, refuse to be deceived. The air was warped. The window and desk appeared to be undistorted rectangles, but she knew better: her own sight must be equally deranged by the warp in the air. The doctors—and she herself—were weird apparitions contoured by the bend in time, but *here*, clearly, the apparitions were supposed to be the real thing. The words being spoken seemed to make sense, they sounded like her native Japanese, but *here* they were probably a code with a totally different set of meanings. It was up to her to fathom it somehow.

Kōko watched the doctors' lips attentively and listened closely to their voices. She had a sudden sense that her vision and hearing were limitless and perfectly clear. She could see and hear everything. She could even make out the capillaries inside the doctors' mouths.

T-h-e-r-e i-s n-o fetus: these were the first code words that reached Kōko's ears. T-h-e-r-e i-s n-o fetus. Y-o-u a-r-e n-o-t pregnant. Now, what did that mean? The two doctors, taking turns, continued to send Kōko coded messages.

"You are in a physical condition similar to pregnancy, but you're not pregnant. Quite a few women develop this phenomenon, for various reasons. There's absolutely no need to worry, it's not at all abnormal."

"Of course, this will be difficult for you to believe, but you must try to accept the fact calmly."

"To help convince you we'll do X-rays and a pregnancy test, and if you're still in doubt and your condition doesn't change, we can also provide hormonal treatment, for example. We intend to do everything possible to help you fully accept what has happened."

"The female body, unlike the male, is so intricately and delicately organized that it can only be called mysterious. Almost all women's ailments—menstrual problems, morning sickness, miscarriage, the menopause, and even breast and uterine cancer—are deeply associated with the mind."

"In other words, there are many illnesses that simply clear up according to the patient's mental state. Morning sickness is a typical example: there have been cases with actual symptoms so severe that the mother's health was in danger and an abortion had to be considered, but as soon as she entered the hospital and began talking with other patients she got over her depression and was perfectly all right."

"In your case, also, because you believed you were pregnant your body responded with changes which simulated pregnancy. As with morning sickness, the important thing here is the way you feel about it."

"Of course, we can explain whatever you might want to know about the physical aspects. First, when the patient begins to believe she is pregnant, the related hormones are activated, stimulating the uterus and making it swell to a certain extent. Then fatty tissue is stored around the intestines, and the mammary glands also develop under hormonal influence so that the breasts enlarge. In some cases they even produce milk."

"The fetal movements you reported are nothing more than movements of the intestines."

"But I'm sure that you don't want to hear this sort of information in the first place. The main thing is to disentangle your feelings, which have become preoccupied with pregnancy. We suggest you come in for some regular sessions at the psychiatric department here."

"Many people don't like the sound of the words 'psychiatric department,' but of course that's merely a prejudice. We refer many of our patients there for a chat as part of the treatment for the morning sickness and menopausal troubles that I mentioned earlier."

"And so we recommend a course of such visits—nice and easy, like dropping in for a cup of tea—to enable you to accept what has happened in the fullest sense. What do you think?"

"It need involve nothing more than talking about your troubles, your memories, gossip about other people, that sort of thing."

"And our department will have to keep a check on your health for a while. Five months pregnant, I think you said? There's too much fat for five months."

"What this means is that the stress underlying such rapid and major changes in your body suddenly, now, has nowhere to go. This, paradoxically, is an unnatural state which just might result in some slight trouble. You seem to be pretty robust and not prone to illness, so I don't expect there's any risk, but still, just to be doubly sure. . . ."

"That's right. I imagine this must come as a complete shock to you, but it all depends on how you look at it, you know. Every day, here, we have to deal with miscarriages, unavoidable abortions, and stillbirths, so one could say that you've been relatively lucky in that you've had no physical pain."

"All the same, why didn't you see a doctor before? Is it true that you haven't been to a hospital at all?"

"Actually, in a case like yours I'd have expected you to come in sooner than you would with a genuine pregnancy. We can usually identify the problem and put a stop to things at that point, before the patient reaches the condition you're in now. . . ."

Kōko must have remained absolutely composed throughout, so as not to worry the doctors. She managed not to be kept unduly long at the hospital and not to be especially late at the music store. Only one girl of seven had been left cooling her heels. Kōko started on her lesson by rote and continued through to the last pupil of the day, a ten-year-old boy. Nothing special happened. The children sat before the piano, dreamy but stolid, and banged the keys. If anything, Kōko took more care than usual to correct the positions of their soft fingers with the black-rimmed nails.

After work she had dinner in a restaurant and returned to the apartment. The moment she took off her shoes, the strength left her body. She sat awhile on the step that led from the entrance hall, then went into her bedroom and crawled into bed without undressing. But she couldn't seem to get to sleep. Her abdomen was still tender and distended. Nothing had changed: the fact weighed on her mind, it made her head ache. She tossed and turned, moaning aloud. In spite of everything, she couldn't stop lying in a way that favored her stomach.

Anything would have been easier to accept. Her whole body burned with humiliation. She could have stood the sight of anything they might have shown her: a fetus like the lungfish in the aquarium, a fetus like a lizard, even a plain lump would have been better than this. Nothing. How was it possible? What did they mean, nothing? She simply couldn't comprehend.

Nothingness was beyond her ability to grasp. She had once tried to approach the concept of outer space in some fashion of her own, but even before its boundlessness could terrify her it had made her feel sick. She was still in grade school then. It had seemed uncanny that she was actually living within something of which she had only the remotest conception.

That night Kōko's troubled dreams were filled with nebulae which she'd seen illustrated in some encyclopedia. Cancer, the Pleiades cluster, the nebula of Andromeda: countless stars sending a clear light into the purple-tinged ultramarine of space. They were beautiful.

7

Kōko took the next day off and stayed in her room. She didn't go out or see anybody the following day, either.

On the evening of the third day Osada came to see her without telephoning.

"Are you still planning to have it?" he said as soon as he was seated in the kitchen.

Kōko was unable to find a reply, and Osada didn't seem to have expected one anyway for he went on, stumbling over the words:

"The child will be illegitimate, then. . . . That might not matter to the parents, but what about the child itself? Even a divorce upsets the children more than you might think, so it's obvious there'll be some pretty serious hangups involved. . . . But I'll recognize the child if it actually arrives. . . . I'm not happy about any of this, but I'll go that far. I'll pay child support, too, though it won't amount to much. . . . If it's mine I want to do the right thing. . . . "

Osada broke off and looked Kōko in the face. She swallowed painfully and lowered her eyes, but she could tell that he was rubbing fiercely at his nose. So Osada had been brooding over this for three days: the thought unloosed her exhaustion again, and her body seemed to cave in like mud.

". . . You wouldn't discuss it with me when you could have done something about it, no, damn you, you had to leave it till now. . . . Anyway, I can't marry you, but I'm prepared to do my basic duty as the child's father. Since there seems to be no question that it *is* mine, I won't try to duck out of it. . . . Are you listening? What's the matter? Suits you better to keep quiet, does it?"

Osada drew a deep breath and released it softly. They faced each other in an interminable silence. Kōko didn't dare lift her head to see his expression.

How should she reply? She would have given anything to be able to unwind with him, to have a good laugh. What had gone wrong? Though she might have lost a lover, she didn't want to lose Osada as a friend at least—a friend she could meet and share a joke with now and then. Was that impossible? Was it so unreasonable to ask? She saw her sister's eyes again, and Hatanaka's, and Mrs. Doi's. How she had wanted to talk with Doi's wife. But she'd never quite had the courage to make the first move. While she always believed that the pain they both felt would simply dissolve if they could just talk things over, instead she had put together an image of the woman entirely out of guesswork and stormed it with emotions of every kind: hatred, bitterness, contempt.

After a pause—she had no idea how long it lasted—Osada suddenly stood up.

"We'll have plenty of time to talk from now on, anyway. I'll be calling in as often as I can."

Kōko nodded as she got reluctantly to her feet, then followed Osada to the door. When he had put his shoes on, he peered into her face. "You don't look very well. You should try not to overdo it, you know. Oh, yes, what did they say at the hospital the other day?"

For the first time, Kōko reacted: "Nothing special . . . but . . . why do you have to leave? It seems a pity . . . when we haven't made. . . . "

Kōko was at a loss. Under her breath she was asking herself: had they ever really lain in each other's arms? What had there been between her and this man? The question drove everything else from her mind.

"You can't be serious! It doesn't matter how much you want it, you've got to go easy from now on." Osada burst out laughing and laid his hand on her shoulder; Kōko staggered. "You must take it easy, you know, when you're expecting. Anyway, I'll come again soon, if it's all right with you."

With another smile in her direction, Osada departed.

When she closed the door behind him the headache that had been developing while he was there suddenly became unbearable, and she climbed hastily into bed. I haven't eaten properly for three days now, she told herself, her thoughts leaving Osada already. She wasn't hungry—the very idea of food was nauseating. Her stomach was lined with a dull ache and a gassy, bloated feeling, as when she'd once eaten *tempura* fried in rancid oil. Her former appetite must have gone for good; she resented the hospital doctors all the more on that account.

Kōko closed her eyes and curled into a ball. A girl appeared, far off, adrift in the darkness that filled her eyes. It was herself; a child of about ten, sloppily playing Hanon in the tiny sitting room. In the garden poking at earthworms with a twig, with her brother who was back from the forest home, not long before he died of a cold. Standing in a corner of the living room reciting the multiplication tables for her mother, who'd lost patience with her awful arithmetic grades, while her sister snickered. The walk to school along a lane that meandered among temples. With her brother at dinnertime, lifting bits of liver to their mouths one by one, under protest, at their mother's stern bidding.

Kōko was in the third grade when her brother died. After leaving him for three years in the institution, their mother had at last been free enough from other cares to bring him home, and her unfeigned pleasure was so obvious that Kōko was quite put out. She bought him baseball gear, a bicycle, and even a TV set, in the days before everyone had one. His biggest thrill on arriving home, however, was discovering the chicken run in the yard. They must have kept chickens at the institution, because he went to work at once to collect worms. Kōko tagged along after him, fascinated by all his doings. And her brother, with an air of great dignity, assigned her this and that little task. He could call her name distinctly—*Koh-ko!*—not slurring it like the rest of his speech.

126

But quite suddenly he was dead, before he ever settled into the special class he'd begun attending at a city school. During the two years he was at home he visited the institution on vacations and wrote often to its teachers and pupils—though his "letters" consisted of strings of all the simple characters and numbers he knew, followed by a note from his mother giving his latest news.

Being still very young, Kōko had been ready to believe that, like her brother, her dead father might come back one day from a dark forest. Then when she saw and touched her brother's corpse, and saw it transformed to ashes in an urn, she came slowly to realize the meaning of death with a new, deep sense of loss. Neither her brother nor her father would return again from the dark forest. Death meant never being able to see someone again. And Kōko had begun to blame herself for what had happened to them both. If she'd only been a nicer baby, her father mightn't have had to die. If she'd only done what her brother had told her more often. . . . Why, oh, why hadn't she tried harder to please him?

After Kayako's birth, Kōko's mother had once remarked that she wished the baby had been a boy. Since Shōko already had a son, Kōko couldn't understand her mother's disappointment. She told her so and her mother had answered –Oh, but what good is that when her little boy doesn't look like anyone on our side?– Then she'd laughed as the absurdity of what she'd said struck home. As a baby, Kayako had so closely resembled Kōko that Shōko liked to say –She looks as if you produced her all by yourself.–

Her brother died before Kōko had a chance to realize he was a special child. She couldn't tell whether that was a good thing or not. Her sister had always hidden his existence from her classmates and boyfriends, but he had never been a source of shame to Kōko. The world in which he lived was peaceful and free, a fairy-tale world.

She had talked about him once to Doi, and about how, before Kayako was born, it had seemed quite possible that a boy like her brother was on the way. This was partly the natural nervousness of a new mother-to-be, but perhaps anticipation had also played a part. When told the baby was a healthy girl, she had been relieved and dejected in the same instant.

Doi's attitude was: –Then why not give it another try by having mine?–

Kōko had frowned at this breezy remark. –It would be a serious matter, if a child like that actually arrived.–

–Yes, but it'd be all the more lovable.–

When Doi put it so clearly, Kōko could say no more. She was grateful, as her brother's sister. She welcomed Doi's honesty, the honesty of one who'd been raised in a healthy family with both parents, and who now had a healthy, intelligent wife and child of his own, and thus had never learned to count his blessings. At the same time, she couldn't help feeling how meaningless their affair must be for him. Like a child, he simply wanted a peek into a world he didn't know.

That evening, Kayako also came to see her. Kōko's eyes refused to open until Kayako (who must have let herself in with her own key) had prodded her shoulder any number of times. Then she took longer still to comprehend that it was actually Kayako sitting at her bedside.

"What? What are you doing here? It's late. . . . Has something happened?" Kōko sat up in bed. The room was in darkness, but Kayako's eyes were clearly visible, glinting in the light from the kitchen. Silvery slanting eyes. After a while Kayako answered, with a catch in her voice:

"Mom . . . are you going to have a baby?"

Kōko nodded without stopping to think.

"Then it's true. . . . I thought you must be terribly ill. . . . Yesterday, Miho finally told me. I was shocked. Why did you keep it a secret? When I'm the one most concerned. . . . "

As there was nothing Kōko could say, she got up and went into the kitchen. It was not yet nine by the kitchen clock.

Kayako went on excitedly to describe her aunt's touchiness, and all her own forebodings, then she eyed her mother's body uneasily again and broke into little giggles of bewilderment. When she had laughed for a moment or two she stood up, red-faced. "I have to go, I sneaked out without telling anyone. I just had to ask you about the baby.... Are you all right on your own?"

Kōko nodded and gazed at Kayako's face, but Kayako immediately turned her back. "Well, goodbye...."

Though she could tell the child hoped her mother would stop her, Kōko simply saw Kayako out. She was bleary-eyed, with a violent headache.

What mattered right now was to get some sleep. As she was taking a couple of aspirin, she noticed her reflection in the window where she'd forgotten to close the curtains. She studied it, and it returned her gaze. It floated, outlined sharply in the night sky. Kōko stared hard at the figure in growing perplexity.

Four days later, Osada phoned and suggested a meal somewhere. Kōko started to say no, but on second thoughts asked him to come over to the apartment because she wanted to talk. "About seven then, if that's all right," he said, and hung up. Kōko rubbed her belly thoughtfully after putting down the phone: if she wasn't mistaken, the swelling was gradually going down.

I'll never get him to forgive me, will I? With a heave of her shoulders she let out a sigh. She'd spent a week now in a daze, clutching the bedclothes, lost in dreams of childhood scenes. Though she'd done nothing but sleep and eat, the week had slipped by amazingly fast. Eventually, however—for all her efforts to recapture those happy moments from the past—she would have to come to terms with the doctors' judgment. Kōko knew already that there was no way to fight it.

She allowed that the pregnancy had been imaginary: that wasn't the problem. What remained beyond belief was that she had brought it on herself. *Why* would I have imagined I was pregnant, to the point of changing physically? *Me?* I didn't want to get pregnant. I was afraid of it, but I shrugged off the risk; it wouldn't really happen, I thought, not at my age. Then I assumed that this carelessness had led to an actual pregnancy. And once I'd got myself pregnant, I decided—but not bold-

129

ly, no, only with immense difficulty—to try accepting this embryonic life for my own and Kayako's sake; but I was still short of confidence even then, and so I told my sister and—as it turned out in the end —made the fact known to Osada.

She went over what had happened again and again, but it never amounted to anything more. She simply could not see where she might be making a mistake. Since she couldn't understand what had happened, she supposed it must have some wholly foreign cause. The doctors, however, had said that unlike ordinary illnesses this one was a case of self-delusion, pure and simple. It would never have happened if she hadn't thought it was happening. She was like the frog in Aesop's fable who tried to imitate an ox till he blew up and burst. "As big as this? As big as this?" asked the father frog as he puffed up his stomach with great gulps of air. She was certain she hadn't wanted a baby, and yet they told her she'd wanted one so badly that she had puffed up her stomach herself.

Most bewildering of all, these two things had both been real, and *both at the same time*. Neither was a figment, nor a fleeting image. She'd believed, in spending her time the way she did, that this reality was the only one there was; simultaneously, this same Kōko had been pumping air into her belly, wishing her way to pregnancy.... But when had she split in two? She didn't know. And how was she going to piece her two selves back together again? She didn't know. The only time she'd noticed passing had been spent in one way: as a genuine expectant mother.

As she sank deeper into thought, Kōko was attracted again to the hard light, indistinguishable to the naked eye, of the stars scattered in space. Light is time, she thought. Two thousand light years. Five million light years. Thirty-five million light years. Four billion light years. Light is time. Then darkness must be a release from time. Light, and its absence. But was there any darkness where one could truly escape the light? Diffracted light. Refracted light. The stars scattered in their trillions. Time scintillating. Primordial light. Light that preexisted the galactic system. Time that could no longer be called time. . . .

Kōko shifted her eyes giddily from her stomach and breathed deeply. Her gaze swept over the frying pans and bowls on the kitchen shelves; perhaps, she thought, there are some things which the likes of me shouldn't try to understand. There was a pain in her side like a cracked rib: she had never known that such loneliness existed. She realized she hadn't shed a single tear since she went to the hospital. The neglected, soot-blackened pots and pans held Kōko's absorbed gaze.

That evening Osada arrived a little early. Before he had even sat down, Kōko nerved herself to speak:

"Uh. . . . Look, I'm sorry to have caused you so much worry by the way I've behaved. . . . I've been thinking, too, and I've realized I can't reasonably go ahead with it. . . . "

"What's wrong?" Osada's eyes widened. Her mouth still open, but unable to continue, Kōko searched his face.

"What's wrong with you? Are you saying you want an abortion?"

Kōko nodded faintly. "Yesterday, at the hospital. . . . So let's forget it ever happened. . . . "

As she bowed her head in apology, and went on bowing, Kōko herself was startled at the alibi she'd seized on so abruptly—the moment it entered her head, in fact. It seemed she couldn't tell him, after all, that the pregnancy had been imaginary. With luck, she hoped, Osada would be so struck by the pitiful implications of an abortion that he would take himself off, with awe and sympathy for a woman's sex. The very sight of Osada in his denim jacket, ever the reluctant adult, had made her look for cues, testing him for possible excuses. She didn't like doing it, but she failed to see why she should tell him what had actually happened, either.

Yet Kōko had underestimated the working of Osada's emotions. He snatched up her arms and, looking hard at the belly where a growing fetus should have been, he asked her in a low, hoarse voice: "Have you really gone and done it?" Then, leaving Kōko standing, he sat down heavily and remained still for some time, one hand pressed to his eyes.

131

In her alarm at his reaction Kōko turned to the sink and, without thinking, put the kettle on to boil. Liar though she was, she couldn't pile other lies on top of the first in her own defense. The longer Osada remained silent, the more terrifying her lie became, till she felt unable to breathe.

When the water boiled over with a rattle of the lid and a hiss of water meeting the flame, Osada finally raised his head and broke his silence. And as she turned quickly toward him Kōko thought she saw clearly, for the first time, what all this had meant to him. His dark complexion made it difficult to tell, but she saw now that his face was the sickly shade of tarnished metal. His eyes seemed larger, suggesting how sunken his cheeks had become. She remembered how, until very recently, she had sneered at people's failure to notice her pregnancy.

"But how could you get it done so easily when it was so advanced? Didn't you have to stay in the hospital? Even I know that much. . . . You're lying, aren't you? It wasn't yesterday, was it?"

Kōko hesitated, but nodded anyway.

"I see. . . . No, I don't. . . . Sit down, will you, Kōko? It's hard to talk with you standing."

Kōko hurriedly pulled up a chair. Osada, sighing as though it was more than he could bear, glanced away toward the balcony, through the open doors.

"But I don't understand. Was it a week ago? Was that what you went to the hospital for that day? But in that case. . . . "

Just as Osada turned back to face her with piercing eyes, there was a ring at the door. Saved, thought Kōko, as she ran into the hallway; she was trembling so hard that her teeth chattered.

Kayako was standing with her back to the door, wearing a sheepish smile. Kōko's expression startled her. "Mom, what's wrong? What are you looking like that for?" And she pushed past her disconcerted mother into the next room. Blankly Kōko watched her go, then heard them greet each other. There was nothing at all alarming in the sound.

When Kōko, her head reeling, made her way into the room as slowly as she could, Kayako looked around at once from where she was sitting, very correctly, facing Osada.

"Mom . . . you're looking a bit off color. Auntie's worried. She says I've got to come and see how you are sometimes. But I never knew you had a visitor."

Kōko nodded helplessly, a smile fixed on her face. "Don't you remember who this is?"

Kayako darted a timid glance at Osada and shook her head. He told her in his friendliest manner that they'd seen a lot of each other when she was a baby.

"I knew you when you were so high, and I even know that when you were five you used to wet your bed."

Yes . . . so she did: some corner of Kōko's confused brain echoed faintly to his words. For a time, she'd been worried—a commonplace worry, but serious enough—that the girl's bed-wetting might be due to the divorce, or perhaps connected with her relationship with Doi, and once, she remembered, she had consulted Osada—or rather aired her worries to him, for as a bachelor he could hardly be expected to know the answer. Osada had probably reacted by looking very uncooperative and quickly escaping to some other subject. And yet it seemed he hadn't forgotten Kōko as she was then.

She glanced back and forth from Osada to Kayako without their noticing. Her hands were clutched tightly together and her heart was suddenly racing in her breast. How could she think of sending him home still believing she'd had an abortion?

"Mom," she heard Kayako say, "I can't stay long today, either . . . especially since you've got a visitor. I'll come another time."

"Isn't Kaya living here now?" Osada interrupted.

"Right now she's. . . . "

When Kōko faltered, Kayako answered loudly, in her very best voice: "Yes, I am. It's just that today I have to go out for a little while. . . . You see, my mother can't do anything for herself, even though she's going to have a baby. She couldn't possibly take care of it without me."

"I don't really think that's so. . . . " Osada mumbled uncertainly while his eyes sought Kōko's; but she was lost for words, her mouth stuck open. Kayako continued with mounting excitement:

"Ever since I was a child, I've always thought it wasn't any fun being the only one. I always wished we had a baby. So I'm really looking forward to having a little brother or sister. . . . "

"Kayako . . . be quiet a moment." It was all Kōko could do to force the words out. Kayako turned to her mother with an affected expression. "The baby . . . it's gone. So. . . . "

"The baby?" For an instant Kayako almost giggled, then, open-mouthed in shock, she looked toward Osada. He was good enough to meet her eyes.

"In other words, Kaya," he said, "there was a miscarriage, and the baby died. I'm sure you know what a miscarriage is, don't you?"

Kayako nodded.

"It's a sad thing—but it can't be helped."

Kayako nodded again.

"Your mother's still feeling weak, so you'll take good care of her, won't you? She's always done everything she could for you, Kaya, and now it's your turn. . . . "

Kayako's nose reddened about the tip and her eyes glistened. Osada went on talking as soothingly as he could. Kōko took one deep breath after another, unable to make a sound. At last, when Osada paused, her voice emerged.

". . . No, it wasn't a miscarriage, or an abortion."

Why was this feeble tremor all she could manage? Osada's and Kayako's eyes were fixed dubiously on her. If she wasn't careful, a blast of freezing air would rush down her throat when she opened her mouth. But she had to do it just once more. One last time, Kōko told herself as she met their stares.

". . . I was only making myself think there was a baby. That's what they told me at the hospital. In other words it was—you know, what they call an imaginary pregnancy. Isn't it ridiculous? So there's no need for any silly arguments.... That's all. Kayako, you'll tell your aunt, won't you? Well, you'd better be going.... You too, please, Osada ... if you don't mind...."

When she had said all that had to be said, Kōko turned her back on the pair of them, went into her room, closed the sliding doors, and dived into bed. Her limbs were numb, her sight dimmed by exhaustion. All thoughts of Osada and Kayako were gone from her head. She was lying on the bottom now, she decided, and there was only one direction from here: toward the surface. She must survive till she reached it, whatever happened; right now she must nurture the energy to carry her there. Her position reminded her of a shriveled fetus afloat in a glass cylinder of clear culture medium.

She and Doi had discussed test-tube babies once. Doi had said: –The culture medium would have to be perfect, and you'd probably need total darkness as well. But the experiment would be impossible under those conditions, wouldn't it?–

–Yes, but we have no idea whether the womb is absolutely dark or not– Kōko had replied.

–Of course it is, it's pitch-dark.– Doi grinned. –Where could light enter from? Aha, there you go again. Expecting something crude, aren't you? It must be dark—pitch-dark—it has to be.–

Doi's voice came back to her gaily. Kōko tried to remember his profile, as though missing someone long dead, but she'd got no further than the oval outline of his face and the always puffy-looking eyelids when she was enfolded in sleep.

... Kayako was sitting by herself in the kitchen watching TV. She jumped up and went in to Kōko when she noticed she was awake. Half submerged in sleep, Kōko asked: "What are you doing? Have you been here all along?"

"I've just got here. You're always crabby first thing in the morning, Mom, so I didn't like to wake you. I'll serve breakfast, if you'll wait a bit."

"Good grief! What time is it?"

"Let's see . . . a little after eleven."

"In the morning?"

"That's right. Now, you wait there."

Kōko obediently laid her head on the pillow. She felt good—alarmingly so. She shut her eyes again, hearing the television and the clatter that Kayako was making in the kitchen. She'd forgotten how pleasant the faint murmur of a TV set could be—and while she was taking this in she drifted back to sleep.

It was only for a brief twenty or thirty minutes, but as she dozed Kōko dreamed she was sunbathing, lying on her stomach beside a pool. It was the one in the grounds of her college. She had seldom seen anyone but the swimming team use it. Though she'd often thought what a waste it was, Kōko had never swum there either. In the dream, she had the pool all to herself; there was no one about. The water reflected the light so intensely she couldn't keep her eyes open. I wish Kayako had come too, she was thinking. I wonder if I should go and tell her. But Kōko couldn't get up, she couldn't even lift her head, she was feeling so good where she lay.

She heard Kayako's voice.

"Mom, breakfast's ready. . . . It's gone a bit funny."

She found herself back in bed, and sat up. The white kitchen ceiling dazzled like the pool's surface.

Kōko admired Kayako's breakfast more for the beauty of its color scheme than for the way it tasted. She sat down to eat at once, watching the girl's face. The green of the salad. The yellow of the omelet. The red of the ham. Kayako filled a bowl with strawberries and set it in the center of the table. It was all so colorful that the meal had something delightfully bizarre about it. There was a movie once that changed midway into Technicolor, a feat that had amazed young Kōko more than any magic trick.

It was just last night that those two met up, then. Kayako must have come back about half an hour ago, after buying the food at a supermarket earlier in the morning. Something told Kōko that this break-fast was her sister's idea. Still, she couldn't help feeling a little disappointed when her guess was confirmed.

"But don't you have to go to school?" Kōko asked. Little by little the events of the night were coming back. How had Kayako reacted? What had Kayako and Osada talked about afterward?

"Today's a holiday. It's Founders' Day."

"Oh. . . . How is junior high, by the way? Do you think you'll enjoy it?"

"Can't tell yet. . . . "

When she realized she hadn't asked before about life at the new school, Kōko fell silent.

She could almost hear her sister's advice to Kayako:

. . . An imaginary pregnancy is a kind of nervous breakdown, you see. Your mother, poor thing, probably convinced herself that she could forget how lonely she is if she had a little baby to look after. But she'll get over it, all right. We'll just have to be gentle and keep an eye on her. We must get her to come here, whatever we do. Kaya, dear, see if you can persuade her, somehow, though I don't suppose it'll be easy. . . .

Kōko was forced to take another look at recent events: what *had* she been hoping for in trying to have a baby? It was after Kayako moved out of the apartment that she found she was pregnant. Which would seem to prove her sister right. But was that all? She couldn't help thinking she must have missed some vital point, something more than the rift between her and Kayako. What was it she'd expected of the baby? There must have been something.

Kōko tried hesitantly to get Kayako talking.

"Which did you want, a little sister or a little brother?"

Kayako's reply was unexpectedly lighthearted: "A brother, of course."

"Why?"

"Oh, one girl is enough. Girls are no fun."

". . . When you were born, I was hoping for a boy, too. . . . Yes, I felt the same way as you. There weren't any men in my family . . . or there was one boy, but he died young. You know about him, don't you, Kayako? Your uncle, between your aunt and me. I loved him very much. . . . He couldn't talk properly, and his clothes were always dirty, but, well, he was just like a big baby who never grew up. It didn't matter how dirty he got, or that he couldn't do anything. He was such a baby. When I cried because Granny was angry, he'd be concerned and try to comfort me. It was a shock to know he could care so much about other people.

"I loathed piano practice and was always trying to worm out of it. One day I said that hateful piano could fall to bits for all I cared, and he made a mighty effort to pull it over. I only just stopped him by yelling no, don't, you'll get hurt. . . . That's the kind of person your uncle was. When we had a treat he'd let me go first, but, being a pig, I'd help myself to his share as well while he wasn't looking. There would be tears, of course, when he found his helping gone, but I'd look innocent and let him howl. The way I saw it, he'd never figure out what had happened, so I wasn't scared or ashamed. . . . Your uncle was like that. . . . "

Suddenly noticing how talkative she'd become, Kōko checked herself and looked at Kayako. Kayako said nothing, simply meeting her mother's glance with a nod and a smile. Kōko returned uncomfortably to her subject. As her lips shaped the words, the brightness outside kept attracting her attention: it must be an exceptionally fine day. The ceiling rippled with sunbeams cast up by the balcony; they could have been at the bottom of a pond awash with sunlight. The vivid pink of Kayako's face reminded Kōko inescapably of a flamboyant tropical fish.

"It's a long, long time since your uncle died. But whatever I do I don't want to forget him. I wonder why? And I want you to remember too. He was your uncle, after all. And, no matter what anyone says, I was happiest when I was with him. So I wanted you to know what it was like too—even if it wasn't quite the same. I don't know how it would have turned out if there'd been a baby brother for you . . . but that's what I was thinking, without consulting you. . . . "

138

Kayako's bright lips moved and a small voice crossed the space between them.

". . . I'm sure I would have loved him too."

"Mm . . . Knowing you, I'm sure you would," Kōko murmured, her eyes on Kayako's face. "When you were little, though, you wanted a big brother or sister rather than a baby one. And before I knew it you started believing they existed. For a while you were quite insistent that big brother did this and big sister did that. . . . You'd say 'My brother told me to do it' with such regularity that you had even me worried. I thought about taking you to see a specialist, but before I got around to it you gradually stopped. . . . It must have been after you went to school. I know I thought that starting school certainly makes a difference. . . . Do you remember?"

As Kōko smiled encouragement, at the back of her mind she knew that wasn't how it had been. Doi had been behind that big brother business. The child's image of a protector—an older brother or sister—had served to camouflage his connection with her mother; and it had lasted just as long. How careful Kayako had been to avoid the word "father," though, when Doi was still coming to the apartment. The odd remark such as –I've been here with Daddy– might slip out, but would be covered up quickly with an –Oops, I mean Uncle.– –Where does Uncle Doi live? Is Uncle Doi nice?– she would ask. Yes, she was careful, but still the words would tumble out: –Mommy, you mustn't go away and leave me. Does Uncle Doi belong here? Where does he always go? I wish my Daddy would come and see us too.–

Kayako pouted dubiously. "That's funny. . . . You mean, they weren't really there?"

"No, they weren't anywhere. Why? Have you always thought they were real?" Kōko asked in surprise, and Kayako, no less surprised, nodded.

"Because . . . I can clearly remember lots of things. So I thought those two kids must have lived near us. But they didn't?"

"No. They were entirely in your mind."

Kōko stood and went out onto the balcony flooded with white light. They'd tried growing house plants there—Kayako's idea—but they could never remember to water them. The blue pots were still standing in a corner. She could feel the sun's warmth through her clothing. The streets were bathed in the same light, and the blue sky soaked up the street noise. Long ago her science teacher had asked the class why the sky was blue. The sun's light, they learned, can be divided into seven colors, with other bands invisible to the eye. And why is blue the only one of these that we see in the sky? Well, because the air absorbs the others. Blue is the only color reflected by the atmosphere, and that's why the sky is so blue.

Kōko marveled at the warm radiance spread over the scene below. How impartial the light was! It streamed into the tiniest crevices between roofs, missing none. It might go unnoticed by people passing in the street, but it was there. It caught each leaf on the roadside shrubs. There was no shadow without good reason, without some object in the way. Light simply obeyed the physical laws that generated it, dispassionately. Surely nothing else fell to us with such perfect equality? She drew a deep breath at the thought. And yet how strangely it had turned out: there was light; then living things, engendered by light, evolved into the human species; and there, at the end of the line . . . call it petty emotion, or the mind; whatever it was, it was impenetrable to light. Yet this stream was constant and immutable, reaching us every second: that was another thing she didn't understand. . . .

The part of the city she surveyed from the seventh-floor balcony appeared to have changed little in thirty years. There was a surprising amount of greenery: temple grounds, a park, a university campus. Kōko had known the area nearly all her life. Had the influx of light not varied a fraction in that time? Here and there new high-rise buildings towered like tall-stemmed plants above a rolling meadow, glinting in the saturating sunshine. Kōko was dimly reminded of the scale of time in which she stood, of how that unchanging cityscape could be transformed by light at any moment to become an ocean floor, a desert, or a glacial tract. What a sparkling day it was, though! Not a speck of cloud in sight.

Kōko turned to Kayako, still sitting in the kitchen. "Shall we go for a walk?" she said. "It's a shame to be indoors on a day like this."

They spent an hour or so in the park, then, at Kōko's suggestion, strolled into the grounds of the nearby university. There were few people about, though as far as they knew it wasn't a holiday. The green of the old ginkgo trees lining the avenues was crisp and cool. They circled a somber lecture hall and reemerged onto the street behind the medical school.

Kōko, though a student herself at the time, had only seen news photographs of the protests that had torn this campus. She recalled the painful images: the students, skins as soft as babies', pitched against the riot police in their heavy armor. The scenes had gripped her imagination, for she recognized in them a mental image of her own. Those figures, hurling stones when they could only hurt themselves, had conveyed no sense of reality, but in its place she'd felt a bond, a fellow feeling. For Kōko believed that she too was throwing stones, in her own way.

The baby that she'd dealt with alone, without appealing to her friend Doi, had been a stone. Moving away from her mother and sister, living with Hatanaka, getting married and divorced. . . .

Two or three months after they signed the divorce papers, Hatanaka had set his heart on a "modern" relationship in which he and Kōko would remain on friendly terms. He telephoned and wrote to swear that no one else would ever care as much about her and Kayako. Kōko flatly ignored him; she told herself that she wouldn't prove her kindness, her courage, or anything at all by a reconciliation. Rejecting Hatanaka was Kōko's stone. He showed up at her apartment, and when she reluctantly stepped outside, with Kayako, he clutched the child in tears and offered to move to the same neighborhood so they could have their meals together . . . which would be fun, wouldn't it? Kōko turned her back on him and went inside, unmoved. She was only afraid he might give way to violence, afraid enough to half consider the suggestion. But she knew how that would end. She could see him taking such a fancy to the scheme that he'd be settling in with room and board. And now that he'd yielded even his parental rights to Kōko, she couldn't count on him controlling his emotions with any more success than before.

Kōko would not let Hatanaka into her life. She regretted what she was doing to Kayako's father, but that was all. She even moved to a new address without letting him know.

When Hatanaka finally came to see an implacable enemy in Kōko, she heard from him only fitfully, as she'd expected; perhaps he had found some new focus for his energies. By that time Kōko was already with Doi. Kayako, who'd been three when her parents divorced, was five. And both Kōko and Hatanaka had turned thirty.

Tiredness overtook her as they reached the street, and she beckoned Kayako into a glass-fronted coffee shop that happened to catch her eye.

There, Kayako revealed how her aunt had been urging her, for nearly a month now, to take the exam for late admission to the private school. Kayako had plainly been worrying herself as to whether it would be wrong to refuse. Kōko listened without interest or attention, however. She had already given her answer as Kayako's mother, and there was nothing more to say on the subject. From Kayako's point of view, Kōko decided, she was simply her mother: no more, no less. Nothing would alter the fact, but nor could Kōko bind her daughter to her as her very own.

Nursery school days. Her grandmother's ways. The neighborhood park. The bean-throwing ceremony at a local shrine, and the summer festival. The record of a TV theme song that she wanted played over and over again. The stuffed toy she never put down. The time Kōko was laid up with a cold. Kayako's bouts of chicken pox and mumps. . . .

They'd slept together in the bed that Hatanaka left behind. It had been just this time of year. Next to the bed was a window which Kōko would open first thing in the morning, and Kayako would spring out of bed, stung by the cold. With a quick greeting they'd run shivering to the kitchen to dress in front of the gas fire. Then, grabbing a few bites of toast, they would rush out of the apartment. Kōko left Kayako at the nursery on her way to the ballet school where she worked as accompanist. And in the afternoons she went on to a private kindergarten where she taught piano. Both were well-paid jobs that Michiko had found her.

In theory, her days ought to have been twice as busy once Hatanaka was gone, and yet it was the carefree mood of those early mornings that lived on in her memory. Every day was wrapped in the faint warmth of the blankets they'd slept in, snuggling together. There was no one they had to be frightened of waking. They could bounce on the bed, crow –Good morning, good morning, rise and shine!– or throw open the kitchen window and swing into their exercises, puffing steamily.

Hatanaka always went to bed toward dawn. He could only concentrate at night, he said, and then only after twelve. He would watch the late shows, fix himself a midnight snack of instant noodles, and reread the newspaper before he sat down at his desk. He was preparing to take the state law examination for the fourth time. *This* year he was going to pass, he claimed, but Kōko never took it seriously. Nor, most likely, did he. Much of his time was spent writing long letters to old friends or reading novels.

–Why won't some other line of work do? I've got a lawyer for a brother-in-law already. Why don't you leave that sort of thing to him?– Kōko said to Hatanaka after his third failure, when she couldn't stand it any more. Hatanaka frowned up at her.

–That's easy for you to say, with one in the family. Lawyers are an elite, they get respect, people call them "sir."–

During the last year of their marriage Kōko would creep into the kitchen carrying Kayako and help her out of her pajamas with much whispering and shushing. If Kayako woke Hatanaka, Kōko would dread what was to follow like an encounter with a ghost. More often than not, Hatanaka would merely trudge to the toilet, his face sallow from lack of sleep, and back to bed again. Sometimes he mumbled in passing: –You leaving already? Sorry to be always like this.– And Kayako would reply: –Sleep tight, Daddy.–

By then Kōko couldn't look directly at him. After this life had dragged on for some time, Hatanaka took Kayako with him on a visit home, saying he needed the rest. At that point Kōko sensed vaguely but undeniably that the current in which she and Hatanaka were both immersed was about to divide. She realized, too, that she wasn't anxious on that score, but only at the thought of losing Kayako. Though she was shocked at her selfishness, one thought—that she wouldn't part with Kayako—was all that gave Kōko the strength to go on speaking civilly to Hatanaka. When he moved out he left Kayako with her as a matter of course. But she could never believe that her fears had been unfounded.

One morning, soon after she and Kayako began their life together, they were woken by piercing cold. There was an unearthly brightness in the room. Kōko threw open the window to see everything below her lightly coated by the still-falling snow. Tire chains crunched in the distance. White siftings piled along the power lines, and patches were sliding to the ground from the neighbors' tiled roofs.

–Kayako! It's snowing!–

Rubbing her eyes, Kayako propped her face on the windowsill.

–Wow, it's snowing, it's snow, Mommy!–

They stayed by the window to gaze at the powdered street, then they dressed quickly, drank down glasses of milk, and ran outside. Large flakes were drifting steadily from the sky like balls of lint. Kōko and Kayako trampled happily on the inch-deep layer, watching their footprints turn instantly to slush, until it was time to leave for nursery school. Tramping was the only way to enjoy so light a fall.

After midday the snow turned to rain and all traces of white vanished from the streets. That afternoon, however, Kayako ran a high fever. Kōko, at work at the kindergarten, received a phone call from the nursery asking her to come for her child. She felt momentarily dizzy when she remembered her own excitement of the morning; it was frightening, the way she'd cheerfully let Kayako play in the falling snow.

Belated anxiety clutched at her: could she really bring up Kayako by herself?

When Kayako was quite better and Kōko could stop worrying long enough to take in her surroundings, she found that spring was upon them. It was March, and the first sweet daphnes were out. Kōko bought a potted primrose and a bunch of marguerites. They gave her such pleasure when she brought them home that she took one deep breath after another and still wasn't quite satisfied. Somehow it wasn't enough that Kayako shared her delight; all at once she saw the loneliness of an adult and a child—one of each—gazing at the flowers.

When Doi began to visit the apartment, for the first two or three months Kōko would move from the bed she shared with Kayako to his mattress on the floor for the middle hours of the night. But after a while she began to have Kayako sleep alone in the bed, even when Doi wasn't there. . . .

Kōko was conscious of a question growing at the bottom of her belly in place of the baby: why did she go on living still? There was no justification, none. The same thought had often haunted her as a child. After her brother's death she'd wondered why she had to stay alive when, whichever way she looked at herself, there wasn't a single redeeming feature to be found. They were wasting the food and clothes they gave her, and the place at school. The more she thought about it, the less reason she saw to carry on. Yet she made no attempt to die; and this very fact added to her humiliation. Dying was too frightening, after all, to be seriously contemplated. The closest she could come to it was gazing down on the school playground from the rooftop, or fingering a bottle of some poisonous reagent in the science lab.

Kōko was shaken by the realization that even now, more than twenty years later, she still lacked any compelling reason to go on living. And by the fact that the will to live was still there.

8

Kōko returned to work after two weeks' absence. The Golden Week holidays of early May were already close at hand. As soon as she set foot in the office she found herself in trouble for failing to contact them, though in actual fact one of the staff, worried when she didn't appear, had phoned her on the very first day. Although Kōko couldn't even remember the call, it had given her a chance to tell them that she was feverish and ill, too ill for just a cold. No one doubted her story when they saw her looking a little on the thin side.

"It seems to have been the flu. I'm fine now," said Kōko reassuringly in the office and the practice rooms.

That evening, she returned the keys on her way out, then crossed to a department store on the opposite corner of the intersection. She took the escalator to the third floor and made her way to the department on the right, where the first thing that met her eyes was a white rattan cradle, then a red crib, a mesh playpen, walkers and baby carriages. Beyond them she could see mannequin babies in various poses on top of the display cases. The floor was not busy, since it was nearly closing time. In one corner, in the baby clothes section, a very pregnant young woman and a middle-aged saleswoman were loudly discussing articles of white fabric, holding them up and discarding them one by one. From the maternity dress section close by, where she pretended to be making a choice, Kōko strained to catch what they were saying. The customer seemed undecided between Western- or Japanese-style diapers; the saleswoman was very much in favor of the Japanese kind.

Kōko's mother had made Kayako's diapers from old cotton *yukata* that she picked apart and ran up on her machine. -You should really be sewing these yourself- her mother had sniffed, -and praying for your baby's health with every stitch.- When Kōko began bottle-feeding Kayako almost at once, her mother had used the same tone: -What do you mean, you've no milk? I've never heard of such a thing. What do you think your baby is, giving her cow's milk? You haven't even tried massaging, have you? When I had you—in wartime, mind, during the evacuation—I massaged my breasts and worked desperately hard at feeding you.-

-But that was then- Kōko said, and took no notice. In fact she hadn't been interested in knowing what went on when she was a baby. She hadn't asked her mother, or her sister either, and then her mother had died before she could get the facts straight. No one had thought the end would come so soon; she herself had probably expected to live another twenty years, at least. Kōko missed her chance to find out where her brother had been looked after, why he was left in the home instead of returning with the family to Tokyo, why her father (who taught music) wasn't evacuated with them, what had happened while he stayed behind in Tokyo—or, more importantly, what kind of person he had been. While in junior high she did sometimes ask her sister, but though Shōko was seven years older her memory of it all seemed hazy, too. Some things must have left a lasting impression, but she wasn't keen to talk about them. There was no point in dragging out what was long past. And, except where their brother was concerned, the two sisters had shared the same outlook as they grew up and raised children of their own.

"Auld Lang Syne" signaled it was closing time. The customer at the babywear counter bought Japanese diapers and took the escalator down. The staff were flipping cloth covers neatly over the display cases and mannequins. A plain young woman with heavy pink lipstick came briskly over to the maternity dress section when she noticed a customer still standing there.

147

"Excuse me, madam. . . . "

As the customer turned to face her, she blushed and left off in mid-sentence. The older woman's eyes were bloodshot and the sides of her nose wet. Before the saleswoman could say a word, the weeping customer drew herself up and strode over to the escalators, not bothering to brush the tears away. The escalators were both going down, and had been for a long time.

She rode to the first floor. As she walked along the aisles, between counters draped with pale olive cloths, a dread of being trapped alone overnight in this huge empty building began to grow so fast that she couldn't keep pace. Kōko took a small pride in refusing to break into a run for the exit, even then, and walked deliberately on at her normal pace.

When Kayako learned that her mother was back at work, she watched for her outside the store every few days. On each of the three holidays during Golden Week she arrived at the apartment with an armful of groceries. They passed the time together at movies and bargain sales. Once the holiday week was over she stood patiently waiting by the store window every evening, smiled shyly when her mother appeared, and walked at her side, never the first to speak. Since she came in casual clothes and without her satchel, she must have been home first to her aunt's. Embarrassed, but a little exhilarated all the same, Kōko took Kayako to a variety of restaurants. She retold harmless stories of the past, and when they'd both eaten their fill they walked together to the station and parted there, Kayako taking the subway and Kōko the train.

Not long after they'd fallen into this routine, Kōko received a phone call from Osada. He had to see her, he had something special to say. Kōko agreed doubtfully. Of course she'd rather not have seen him again if she could avoid it—but she hadn't even apologized to him yet. She couldn't imagine what kind of reparation Osada would seek as the father of the vanished baby. Perhaps he was brooding more deeply than ever because it had been a false alarm. . . . If Doi could see them, what fun he'd have. Ah! so human existence is more abstract than we thought, is it? There's hope for you yet, you know—a fertile imagination, yes, not bad at all. I never knew you had it in you. . . .

You're talking as though it had nothing to do with you. Kōko answered her imaginary Doi without thinking, then felt a sudden chill. It *was* nothing to do with Doi, from his point of view. The baby was hers and Osada's. The baby itself might have been an illusion, but she'd never gone so far as to make Doi the father. She may have wished he was, with ever-deeper regret, but she'd never lost sight of the fact that the baby's father was Osada. It was the ease of her connection with Osada that had sustained her, her lack of attachment to him that had encouraged her; while her eyes, as always, were on Doi.

Kōko was thinking the same thoughts on the way to meet Osada, the following evening.

They'd arranged to meet at a restaurant, quite a large charcoal-grill place. As she stood in the doorway searching the tables, Osada appeared from the farthest corner and led her back with him. There was a man already seated at the table that he pointed out. For a second it struck her as odd that he'd brought a friend, and then she realized it was Hatanaka. She was shocked to think she hadn't recognized him at first sight. But what was this all about? She couldn't keep from glancing inquiringly at Osada. Unawares, Osada walked up to the table and spoke to Hatanaka.

"Well, how'd it be if we get her to sit here and we sit opposite?"

Hatanaka raised his eyes and rested them on Kōko. For an awkward moment she hid behind Osada's back.

"Well, go on, move over." At Osada's prompting, Hatanaka slid across to the next seat.

"She's looking well," she heard him say.

"She is, isn't she?" Osada settled himself in the vacated chair. Losing her hiding place, Kōko gave a deep, flurried bow which kept her face hidden as she accepted an empty seat. She could hear an impatient voice inside her crying: quick, you must greet them with perfect poise.

149

But how?—when Osada, as well as Hatanaka, was watching her as though she were a cat who'd tumbled around in heat till her fur was worn to mangy patches. She couldn't even look them full in the face, but cowered, and breathed with difficulty. This didn't make sense: why was she reacting like this? There had been doubts and misgivings when she slept with Osada, and again when she believed she was carrying their child, but there'd been no fear of Hatanaka, the man who brought them together. She had never even considered what Hatanaka would think if he knew of their affair. Over the years Hatanaka had dwindled to a figure from the past; the little weight he'd once had as her ex-husband had almost gone.

Surely Osada had long since ceased to regard her as his friend's wife. And yet what was this rush of shame as they sat eyeing her? Had she done anything to deserve the looks of pity verging on abhorrence that they combined to give her after all this time? They hadn't said anything aloud, though; perhaps this suffocating humiliation was just her own childish pique, and a bright smile would set them all at ease. She must snap out of it; but her heart was pounding more and more violently. She could hear voices ringing in her ears. They'll sleep with the first man who comes along when they're on their own. It looks that way, doesn't it? Anyone will do. I've known a lot of women, but I can't handle them when they're like that. Then she gets high and mighty, swears she'll see it through and keep the child herself—and look at her now! That's women for you. You're right. There's no stopping them when they start to slide. . . .

Mingled with their voices, she heard something that Hatanaka had once said. It was when he was seeking a separation, and insisting how deeply he loved her. -You probably didn't know, but I've made more than one woman get an abortion before now, for your sake and Kayako's.- This, he seemed to be saying, showed how much he'd always loved them both, and how hard it would be to leave them, and yet he must, he had to make a fresh start in life; if he stayed where he was it would finish him.

–I've left women, too, for your sake. I was thinking of you and Kayako all along. But now you don't seem to need me any more. It's time you lived your own life, anyway. You don't have to let me drag you down. Your family has money. I'll be penniless from the day I leave. But I'll survive somehow, you'll see. And I won't forget you two. I'll never love another woman, I know.– Sometimes Hatanaka would be moved to tears.

But it had made Kōko's flesh creep to hear him offer these proofs of his love—the women he'd left, the children he wouldn't let them have. Could she really have been prepared to stay with a man like that all her life? It had given her a pang of concern for that unknown young woman whose existence, but no more, had become obvious from phone calls and letters. She felt a certain guilt that went with being one man's wife.

The legal proceedings followed over a year later, but she was already indifferent to Hatanaka by the time he wanted a divorce. His good looks made his narcissism especially hard to miss. When Kōko reflected that she was one of the reasons for his complacency while she remained his wife, she couldn't stand it a moment longer. She could never forgive Hatanaka: a man who'd tell his wife unashamedly—no, with pride—that he had made another woman get rid of a baby.

–I can't take this life any more, though you don't care, do you? Why the silent treatment? Screw you and your gloomy looks! I'd like to hear some laughter around here, I want to enjoy life, I like women who make a man feel wanted. Come on, say something, if you've got anything to say! There's any number of women just waiting till I'm available. You've never tried to share even one of my problems, have you?–

Hatanaka had put Kōko on her guard against emotion in others. Nothing was harder to handle. Like honey, the sweet flood, once begun, would soon engulf him, clogging his eyes and ears. He was trapped, though in his own mind at least he seemed to glow with beauty through the amber liquid. What visions might its sweet intoxication bring? Many a time Kōko had reacted seriously to something he had said, only to hear him flatly contradict it later; after much confusion she eventually learned to pay as little attention as she would to a child's fibs. Yet she had to admit there was resonance and fluency in the words borne on that torrent of emotion.

When she took up with Doi again, seeing him every few days, what attracted her most was his way of seldom revealing his emotions. At one time—before Doi's first child was born—Kōko's patience had often been tried for lack of clues to his feelings; after Hatanaka, she felt affection for the very same reason. His expression was as elusive as ever; he could as easily have been laughing or falling asleep. He was a good talker as long as he was flippant, but when the subject turned at all serious not a word could be got out of him. Certainly he didn't make theatrical vows of love, but neither did he rise to the most outrageous taunts she could sling at him. Hatanaka, she thought whenever this happened, would have stormed out and never come back, and mixed with her disappointment in Doi she would find a new confidence in him.

Reassuring though Doi's calmness was, it wasn't long before Kōko had grown impatient and excitable, recklessly indulging her own emotions. And the more she did this in front of him, the greater her shame, which only drove her to more hysterical abuse, to tears of vexation. Still Doi ignored her outbursts. It was clear he wasn't going to lose his head and move in with her, but neither would her emotional upheavals keep him away. Doi didn't change, whatever she said or did. He came to see her as steadily as ever.

Doi, she realized, valued his responsibilities more highly than his own emotions. Spectacular collapses were not for him. Though this made him very attractive, in actual fact—since she was neither wife nor sister—emotion was all there was between them. Perhaps they could simply have enjoyed its affirmation in sex, but Kōko began wanting Doi to do more, after all, in irresponsible and foolish ways, until his imperturbability finally became unbearable. With her own emotions in turmoil, feeling at a constant disadvantage, it was hardly surprising that she hadn't been able to have a baby.

What a fool she'd been. Why did everything go so wrong?

But what on earth was Hatanaka doing here? It was three years since she'd seen him last. Under an expensive-looking brown suit he had filled out an inch or two. He had always liked to dress well, and now he wore his smart suit with perfect ease; Kōko hated to admit it (perhaps, she thought, the good taste was his wife's) but he looked impressive, without a trace of cheap flashiness, however sourly she inspected him. She supposed anyone would want to take a second look. In fact his air of distinction dazzled even Kōko momentarily.

She used to think, when they were married, that at most the odd college girl or housewife, not knowing any better, might be taken in by his looks; granted he wasn't bad-looking, but no one with any judgment could miss the hint of meanness in that face. It had been just like him to buy a tailor-made suit and a leather coat when they could barely afford the monthly gas bill. She hadn't protested, though; she'd merely put her mind to choosing a tie to match. She was like a mother wanting her son to look his best: if he must pay so much attention to his appearance, she often thought, then I wish he'd at least dress well. While he was living with her, though, for all the pains he took and all the money he spent, he'd never managed to look anything but slight and immature.

Hadn't she seen what was right before her eyes? Or was it that she'd been holding him back? Eight years had passed. To Hatanaka she was probably an ugly memory returning as a sorry shadow of herself to congratulate him on his present happiness. He would know by now that she'd wanted to have a child with Osada. But he would also have heard, of course, that it had been an imaginary pregnancy. Imaginary pregnancy. The words alone must have made him laugh.

Osada ordered extra food for Kōko and filled their three beer glasses. An assortment of *sashimi*, prawns, and other dishes was already on the table.

"It's been a while." Hatanaka finally spoke directly to Kōko. "I didn't know what to expect, either, but here I am anyway."

Glancing at Osada, Kōko asked him quietly, "Then, you. . . ?"

153

Osada nodded and smiled. "I asked Hatanaka to come an hour early."

She wanted to find out why, but suddenly lost her nerve.

"How's Kayako?" Hatanaka asked, clasping his hands and sounding like a court-appointed counselor.

Kōko fell into the deferential tones of the interviewee: "She's fine."

"Good. She must be at junior high school by now."

"Yes, she's grown quite tall, too."

"And my eldest's just turned three."

". . . Really?"

"Are you still teaching piano?"

". . . Yes."

Kōko's order of grilled prawns and fish arrived.

"Better eat it while it's hot," said Osada. Kōko nodded and took up her chopsticks. She was cursing her own timidity. She had nothing to be ashamed of, so why this shrinking? Anyone would think she was begging forgiveness for her sins. She had to pull herself together, if only by a hearty show of appetite. They were both watching the movements of her chopsticks. Kōko took two mouthfuls of fish and a long swallow of beer. She looked back at them with the glass at her lips. Osada straightened under her gaze and opened his mouth, while Hatanaka started to pick apart the prawns on his plate, smiling slightly to himself.

". . . Actually, I didn't want to take this any further without Hatanaka here, which is why I've asked him along."

Kōko nodded in silence. She was concentrating on the hand that held the chopsticks, determined not to let it shake.

"I've already told him the whole situation, so it's all right."

What does he mean, all right? Kōko muttered to herself.

"It hasn't taken you long, though, has it? You seem to be almost back to normal. . . . It's hard to believe without having seen her, but she was way out to here. Anybody would have said she was pregnant." Osada made a circle with his arms to show Hatanaka, who nodded and raised his glass.

"You don't seem too impressed, but it's quite serious, from what I understand. . . ." Osada turned toward Kōko. "I've done some reading. And asked a few questions—just casually—of a psychiatrist friend of mine. . . . It seems to vary from patient to patient. Some will go on insisting that they're pregnant in spite of all the evidence, and I'm told the doctors will even fake an abortion in such cases. Apparently, imaginary pregnancies don't follow simply because the woman wants a child. When you look into the background, you'll always find some block, some unsolved problem between the man and the woman. . . . "

Osada broke off and, with his eyes on Kōko, lifted his beer glass to his lips, .

". . . And?" Kōko prompted in a barely audible voice. She couldn't see what he was getting at, but her growing uneasiness was now a pain in the pit of her stomach. Hatanaka continued to sip his beer in silence.

". . . And, well . . . forget about the other cases. It's us that matters."

"Us?"

"Yes, us. You're not in this alone. If it was an ordinary pregnancy —but we needn't go into that, because it wasn't. . . . I'm talking about the question of responsibility. I used to think you were different from other women, Kōko. I mean that in a good sense—that you were strong. Of course you *are*, but you have a weak side, too, and I always avoided getting involved with that side of you. I didn't want complications, you see. Only this time, whatever you might *say*, Kōko, what your body has done has given you away. . . . A phantom baby. You remember the other day I said I'd acknowledge it? I meant what I said, of course, and I hadn't ruled out the idea of marriage, either. . . . But it wasn't a true pregnancy. So why don't we lay it decently to rest and make a fresh start, the two of us? I won't take you at your word any longer, Kōko. You're bluffing. . . . And I've got to compromise, too, at my age. . . . And so I thought the first thing was to talk to Hatanaka, which explains why he's here. It's important that he understands."

"Why? . . . If it concerned Kayako, yes, maybe—but why in this case?" Kōko had managed to speak out at last. Braced by the sound of her voice, she sat up very straight.

155

Hatanaka answered her gently. "It does concern Kayako, as well. In other words, Osada is. . . . We're old friends from way back, you see, and in meeting you he was doing me a favor—providing a neutral zone. And so he wanted me to understand before he set things straight with you. Because on paper, anyway, Kayako will become Osada's child. . . : "

". . . What do you mean? What are you talking about?"

Kōko could tell that the blood was rushing to her face. She was ready to scream, to flail her arms, to smash everything in sight. Hearing Osada's voice, she watched his mouth move while she gripped her hands beneath the table and fought the impulse down before it drove her to extremes. She had to go cautiously now or she'd step right into a trap.

"Perhaps 'understand' is the wrong word—I wanted to discuss it with him. Kaya is at a difficult age, for one thing. . . . And you know, Hatanaka said something really helpful: it's true that the parent-child bond is absolute in biological terms, but in social terms it's more relative. And, uh, then he said that the relation between the parents, which forms the child's environment, is a contractual agreement based on their mutual wishes, and they both have the right—and the duty—to seek a more ideal relationship. Which means that if they renounce their right to choose, and with it the chance of giving the child a better environment, then they stand to lose their self-respect. That was the gist of his lecture, anyway. The point is that Hatanaka has no objection to my acting as Kaya's father. Am I right?"

Hatanaka nodded repeatedly, expansively. Kōko remembered and gritted her teeth: this was the Hatanaka she couldn't endure. Eight years hadn't made him any more sensible to shame. And he could talk of self-respect! But there was something else that made her ache all the more to get away; for she'd been reminded of a time when, anxious to secure Doi firmly by her side, she had harangued an invisible audience day and night with precisely the commentary that she'd just heard quoted by Osada.

Hatanaka's relaxed voice took up the theme.

156

"What it comes down to is how we understand love. The trouble is that Japanese society doesn't distinguish clearly between parental love and the marriage relationship itself. And that leads to far too much unhappiness. The important thing is for both the father and the mother to show the child that they love someone. Children whose parents hate each other grow up not knowing what love is, that's the tragedy of it. . . . "

"Look . . . Osada, what did you want to see me about?"

Hatanaka had been about to say more, but he chuckled at the firmness of Kōko's tone. "You haven't changed, have you? There's no need to snarl at us, when it's you who's causing all the worry. I know you, you can't stand people being nice to you."

". . . Will you please tell me at once."

She felt a cold shiver; it set her hair on end. Despite the hard look she gave him, Osada had turned, smiling, toward Hatanaka, who spoke again.

"You must know by now, surely."

"But nothing definite has been said yet. . . . "

"Nothing definite? Trust a woman. Still talking like a starry-eyed girl. . . . Come on, Osada, you sure you haven't changed your mind? Maybe it's not too late. It beats me why you have to be so conscientious. You're a loser, a born loser."

"I'm just doing things in my own way. . . . " Osada gave his tipsy friend a slap on the shoulder and finally looked Kōko in the face. His smile stiffened.

"Fair enough," said Hatanaka. "Right, then, shall I pop the question for you? I've already proposed to her once. . . . This is going to be kind of strange."

"Propose?" Kōko murmured the word as though all her strength had deserted her, and dropped her eyes to the table. Hatanaka laughed his high-pitched laugh again, the way he did when he was in a good mood. At one time the housewives in their apartment building had come to Hatanaka for dancing lessons. Every one of them, in her embarrassment, would tuck her head down and trip over her own feet. And that laugh of Hatanaka's would ring around the tiny apartment as he guided each carefully through the steps. When the neighbors had all gone home, Hatanaka would take Kōko in his arms and murmur –What a bunch of old hens! Not a real woman among them.–

"You seem surprised. . . . At least it's not an unwelcome surprise. And Kayako should get along well with him, too. He's a good fellow, you won't find many like him. Don't look so down in the mouth, though—you'll hurt his feelings."

Osada snapped "Just keep quiet, will you?" as he tried to interpret Kōko's expression. At the same moment she scraped her chair back and was on her feet almost before she knew it. She had to say something quickly, but it was all she could do to struggle for breath. The room was blurred.

"The toilet?"

It was Hatanaka's voice. Kōko shook her head and whispered quickly, "You've got it all wrong. . . . "

"No, I don't think so. Sit down, anyhow." Osada spoke gently, his fingers touching Kōko's hand. She brushed his warm, damp fingers away and went on, looking steadily at the gleam of the beer bottles and glasses on the table.

"You know, if you'd said the same thing to me a year ago, I might have shown the gratitude you seem to expect—I might have jumped for joy. But now . . . no. . . . I'm afraid I've been a nuisance, Osada. I came today to apologize. But . . . it's not going to work out as you planned. . . . You won't catch me playing your buddy-buddy games, you two. . . . I'm going home. You can go on with your cozy chat. . . . "

On trembling legs Kōko turned from Osada and Hatanaka and walked away.

She heard Hatanaka calling. She walked on without looking back. She heard Osada's voice and her arm was tugged from behind.

"Come on, calm down. Don't be so touchy."

Bringing all her strength to bear Kōko prized her arm free from

Osada's grip, beat his grasping hands off with a switch of her shoulder bag, and walked on again.

After a moment she heard him say: "How much longer are you going to put on this act? You're not fooling anyone, you know."

Kōko plunged ahead, bumping into waiters and customers, chairs and tables, her eyes only on the glass doors to the street. How could she have come here, unarmed and unsuspecting? But it will never happen again, she told herself, and by letting her chagrin rule her she managed—barely—to get out without looking back.

The moment she stepped outside a moan escaped deep within her throat, and warm water brimmed in her eyes. She paused to glance up and down the street under its bright neon glare, then set off to the right as fast as she could walk. Perhaps three times tears tracked her cheeks like beads of summer sweat. Osada and Hatanaka did not come after her now. She'd be seeing them again in any case, since Hatanaka was Kayako's father. She had no intention of sneaking about avoiding them.

A boy aged five or six was firing a toy machine gun by the entrance to an alley of bars. Kōko stopped, for the first time since she left the restaurant, and watched him. It was strange to come across one so young among these nightspots: she felt as if she hadn't seen a child in years. When he pulled the trigger the gun barrel flashed a brilliant red and rattled, ratatat-tat. He was aiming at nearby trash cans and lamp-posts and firing in bursts, taking a dramatic stance each time. He had large ears and large eyes.

Soon the gun's muzzle, in search of its next target, swiveled toward Kōko. There was a moment's hesitation, then the boy struck the same pose and opened fire. Rat-tat-tat-tat, came the pleasant clattering sound.

"Aaargh, got me." Kōko twisted and slumped to the asphalt.

The firing stopped. She opened her eyes a fraction, to spy the boy dangling the machine gun and staring openmouthed at her body. As Kōko remained motionless, stifling her laughter, the boy edged gingerly toward her and prodded her back with the gun: still she played dead. Next he caught up her outstretched arm on the tip of the barrel and let

159

it drop. Kōko just lay there, face down.

The boy crouched beside Kōko's body, cradling the machine gun.

"This is weird. . . . She's not supposed to die for real. . . . Hey, it ain't my fault if she goes and dies. Nobody ever died before. . . . "

Kōko's shoulders started to quiver.

"Hhh-hhh-hhh-hhh," Kōko uttered gruffly as she rose, very slowly, from the ground. Stretching both arms toward the boy, who was staring in astonishment, she grappled him to her breast.

"*Hhh-hhh-hhh. . . . Resistance is useless. I have come for you from the farthest reaches of outer space. . . . You are needed. You will surrender, Earth Child. . . .* "

For a brief moment the boy, not knowing what had hit him, let himself be squeezed, but then his whole body expressed a terror so strong it took her by surprise as, head tossing, arms and legs thrashing, he tried to break free. With clenched teeth Kōko pitted her strength against his desperation. He writhed harder and harder, he was all violence—and yet he didn't yell for help.

He wasn't one of those children who ran to an adult for protection the moment anything hurt or frightened them. The thought made Kōko want to hug him all the more. But she couldn't think how to get through to him—and all she asked was that they keep on playing, like a couple of children, unaware of time passing.

Moments later, the boy abruptly stopped lashing out and stood still. Panting, he said: "All right. . . . You win. . . . Just quit hurting me. . . . You're *hurting* me. . . . "

With a rueful smile she slackened her embrace—and quick as a mouse the boy was off. Raising a cry that was half wail, half scream, he disappeared deep into the bar-lined alley as fast as his legs could carry him.

Kōko was too stunned to move. *I wonder if he truly believed I came from outer space. If he did—if he's that kind of child—he'll grow up with a memory of how the being came after him. A genuine creature from outer space in the guise of an earthling. Though one day he may* begin to suspect that he merely dreamed it long ago.

Even if the boy didn't believe me, she thought, at least I'm going to play my part out.

After inhaling slowly, Kōko leveled her gaze at the many-colored bar signs, gradually extended a pair of long silver antennae from the top of her head, and began to beam electromagnetic waves from their tips to the boy, wherever he'd got to. Becoming every inch a space creature for his sake, she made the two antennae vibrate with minute precision.

"That's not fair. So you're a child who breaks his promise, are you? A cowardly thing to do.... I'm very disappointed.... Now I don't suppose I'll ever see you again ... when we could have shared so much joy.... I shall return to my own galaxy.... Are you receiving me? ... Receiving me? ... Receiving? ... "

Kōko stilled the vibrating antennae and concentrated with closed eyes for a little while. There was no reply from the boy. She opened her eyes and turned to face the main street, where a line of cars was waiting at a stoplight. Their countless tail lamps tinged the air with a faint red glow.

Rubbing her eyes, Kōko began to walk along the faintly tinged pavement.

The Women's Press is a feminist publishing house. We aim to publish a wide range of lively, provocative books by women, chiefly in the areas of fiction, literary and art history, physical and mental health and politics.

To receive our complete list of titles, send a stamped addressed envelope. We can supply books direct to readers. Orders must be pre-paid with 60p added per title for postage and packing. We do, however, prefer you to support our efforts to have our books available in all bookshops.

The Women's Press, 34 Great Sutton Street, London EC1V 0DX

Shizuko Gō
Requiem

Translated by Geraldine Harcourt

**'I must fulfil the responsibility of a survivor, on behalf
of the dead who cannot speak for themselves; I must
say what should be said and do what should be done'**
Shizuko Gō

The year is 1945. Setsuko is a 16 year old schoolgirl who writes
letters to Japanese soldiers urging them to fight harder. Naomi
is griefstricken because her father is in prison for opposing the
war effort. Amid sickness, starvation and death, the two girls
find comfort in friendship. They argue about patriotism,
honour, democracy.

The firebombing of Yokohama brings destruction beyond
imagination, and the end of their world.

Shizuko Gō herself survived the bombing of Yokohama. She
waited nearly 30 years to write this immensely moving and
powerful novel, which won the Akutagawa Prize, Japan's
premier literary award, in 1973.

'Unforgettable and devastating, a book which the world needs'
Susan Griffin, author of *Woman and Nature*

'It contains the very important message that war is senseless
and can bring no meaning to life' Petra Kelly, the Green Party,
Federal Republic of Germany.

FICTION £2.95
ISBN: 0 7043 3961 7

Hualing Nieh
Mulberry and Peach

Battered by a life of continuous social and political turmoil, Mulberry finally flees her native China and arrives in America, an illegal immigrant relentlessly pursued by the authorities. Unable to resolve the conflicts between her new life and her old, she accommodates them by developing two personalities instead of one. While Mulberry Green clings desperately to her cultural and ethical roots, Peach Pink renounces her past to embrace with terrible vigour the values and ideals of the American way of life.

FICTION £3.95
ISBN: 0 7043 5005 X

Yuan-tsung Chen
The Dragon's Village

At the age of eighteen, Ling-ling refuses to flee the revolution with her wealthy family. She volunteers to work for the land reform programme in the remote north of her vast country, and share in the exhilaration of social and personal change that sweeps the peasant countryside.

'Yuan-tsung Chen brings a piece of modern Chinese history to life' *New York Times Book Review*

FICTION £4.95
ISBN: 0 7043 3865 3